SOLOMON & SHEBA

SOLOMON & SHEBA

FAYE LEVINE

RICHARD MAREK PUBLISHERS
NEW YORK

Library of Congress Cataloging in Publication Data

Levine, Faye.
  Solomon and Sheba.

    1. Solomon, King of Israel—Fiction.
2.   Sheba, Queen of—Fiction.   I.   Title.
PZ4.L6644So [PS3562.E896]   813'.5'4   79-24671
ISBN 0-399-90069-1

Book design by Iris Bass

PRINTED IN THE UNITED STATES OF AMERICA

For HH

CONTENTS

BOOK THE FIRST

SOLOMON'S AMBITION

THE PARTY

THE PARTY WAS AT ABIBAAL'S HOUSE. The retired king of Tyre was just sinking his teeth (mostly real, two gold) into a cake consisting of a layer of fruit soaked with cane rum, a layer of almond paste soaked with palm brandy, and the whole covered with hard amber honey icing.

His fifteen-year old granddaughter was chatting brilliantly with the newly arrived ambassador from Phoenicia's most distant colony: an exotic western coast rich in metals for a monarch's teeth or a girl's anklets. Her bearing was urbane and assured; she and the ambassador were in complete agreement that Tyre was the most sophisticated spot in the world.

The usual scribes were at the sideboard helping themselves to wine, fraternizing with the musicians (viol and psaltery really exciting, but cymbals a touch brassy), and trying to overhear something witty.

"I'm sorry your stomach was not well at sea," the girl was saying with a little laugh, and a charming toss of her head. "I've never been to sea myself." ("Never? How amazing!") "But next time you really must bring us a blue Druid!" Pleased with this remark, the little princess raised a cup of drugged Babylonian wine to her lips, and turned ever so slightly to catch the light from the candelabras on her gown.

The portly ambassador was as much appreciative of the girl as of the city, but the seasickness of his recent journey was not entirely dissipated. So instead of responding at length about the western islands he merely smiled and mopped his brow and took another little cake.

At the end of the well-stocked table a middle-aged man, his face prematurely lined and his hair all gray, was speaking to a younger, long-haired man. Points were being made emphatically, but in low voices; then there were long pauses.

The older of the two was King Hiram, the reigning monarch, son of Abibaal.

The younger, his confidential friend, was chief architect and engineer in this metropolitan seaport, known everywhere as "the other Hiram" as testimony to the power of his art. His widowed mother, a Jew from a border town, had sent him to school in Egypt, where he had learned much among the sacred builders. But he had been a defiant prodigy, and could not accept academic disciplehood for long. Still young, he had returned to his father's adopted city of Tyre.

Tyre, literate and prosperous, was a good place for artists of every kind, and the architect found it easy to work for the Hiramic dynasty. Along the Great Sea coastline dense evergreen forests and gleaming limestone cliffs provided natural materials in abundance. What was lacking could be easily acquired in India, Arabia, Africa, or Spain by a clever merchant marine. Hiram designed wooden altars and worship totems for the thousand cults of Tyre, and adorned them with imported tin, copper, brass, silver, and gold; and constructed around them massive housings of local stone. At these sanctified spots the Phoenicians achieved an exaltation which the building master did not himself, however, share. For in the temples of Hiram the citizens of Tyre made orgiastic love and committed murder; they castrated themselves and they burned their children.

"It would be possible for you to forbid at least the *sale* of children for the purpose of immolation," he was saying now. "That would be a start." His manner was diplomatic. If the architect had a god, it might be geometry. But geometry demanded no sacrifices.

The king placed his wineglass down on the crimson tablecloth, moving it to just the right spot in the row of embroidered monsters. "I told you my father is against it," he said defensively.

The architect's expression did not change.

"But," King Hiram continued, "we can be sure that Abibaal will die soon enough of pigs and mollusks and then I shall be able to take more of your good advice."

A finger bell signaled the presence of a eunuch at the back door. It was a messenger from the Astarte temple in the nearby cosmetics district, who had heard there were visitors of some importance at Abibaal's, and wanted to know whether the king's party would like some Galli sent over.

The king looked at the self-contained architect, frowned slightly, and refused; the messenger bowed and left.

In the center of the party hall King Hiram's daughter was still engaged in teasing the ambassador. Well-coiffed Phoenician women were walking about in twos and threes, listening to the music, avoiding the scribes, admiring the thick and knotty Sidonian admiral alone in a corner. The hydraulics minister from Marib and the Persian agronomist were discussing flying buttresses.

Suddenly a courier in scarlet livery burst through the twin pillars of Abibaal's porch and breathlessly announced the arrival of the king of Israel. The buzz of conversation stopped.

"I've been looking forward to this," said the king to the architect, and took a step toward the door.

Indeed, his curiosity was enormous, for he had pledged himself to a far-reaching alliance with the son of the late King David merely on the strength of David's achievements and a few letters. The other Hiram and most of the guests hung back in deferent anticipation. Only the daughter of the king, all purple self-confidence, walked over to the solitary admiral, and began to speak to him animatedly, as if unaware that anything unusual was going on.

Then Solomon, with a deep sigh, entered the world of old Tyrus, followed by a cluster of bodyguards and courtiers. He was tall and moved with less grace than sensitivity, and with a slight stoop to his shoulders. Beside him and holding his arm was his young wife, the former princess of Egypt, in a brief and elegant dress. She was delighted to be attending a party in this cosmopolitan city. The trip down had been bumpy and boring, and all the chariot driver had wanted to talk about was shields. Her lip curled with centuries of arrogance. Her eyes searched every face.

The Sidonian admiral was having trouble choosing between the princess addressing herself to him and the one who had just walked in. He maneuvered the former around so he could see over her shoulder. He noticed that the queen of Israel wore an Isis medallion on her forehead. He wondered: wouldn't that be a taunt to her husband's IHVHism? No, he thought, Solomon must understand. Letting some of the Tyrian's conversation go unheard, he caught the Egyptian's eye. It was painted in black, thick and precise, like a fish with a long, slender tail. Real class, he thought. He felt some jealousy. Solomon must be a happy man.

The admiral winked at the queen. She turned her head away snappily.

Meanwhile Hiram king of Tyre had embraced Solomon king over Israel. The older man pronounced a long, sonorous, correct, and possibly even sincere greeting, as points of red showed in the younger man's cheeks. Old Abibaal sauntered over too, and shook Solomon's two hands heartily, and sat down again.

In a clear low voice, as his wife's attention wandered, King Solomon replied, "Your friendship is very precious to us, Hiram. Your seamen till the world; your workmen are more skilled in wood than any people; the masons you sent to my father upon the opening up of Jerusalem established the city, and made it strong."

Hiram laughed with pleasure and proposed a toast. They lifted their majestic arms and hands; thick cut wineglasses glinted. To David.

KING DAVID RECALLED

DAVID WAS A BEAUTIFUL MAN. AT THE start of his military career his slender strength and red and white complexion had bested the giant Goliath on the field. For the ironclad Philistine had been smitten with passion at the sight of this graceful shepherd, this seventh son, who stood before him so poised and so balanced, and he had fallen into a fatal fond paralysis, and allowed a pebble to hit him.

The beauty had remained with David as he grew. The shepherd's balance made him a canny warrior, and he had the naturalness and humility that made men want to follow him. As an exile and a guerrilla he fought, among allies and enemies; he bore the armor of his tribes' first king and then, when that king had become psychotic and suicidal, he battled him in the field and succeeded him.

King David was the son of Jesse and a descendant of Ruth the Moabitess who chose her husband's family when the alternatives were even, and of Boaz of the tribe of Judah, and of Tamar, who conceived by Judah when veiled as a harlot on the road in sheepshearing time.

On the throne of all Israel the self-made man performed extraordinary acts. Before him, the leaders of the tribal league had always gone to the Philistines for weapons and the craft of their manufacture, but David secured the necessary technology for his own. Out of Philistia, where he had lived and fought, David took the noble art of ironwork. Spears and shields, and

15

chariots of wood and leather and gold and the invincible iron, emblazoned with sphinxes and David's double-triangle cartouche, blazed triumphant in the sun from Syria to Egypt, and far to the east of the Jordan into non-Jewish lands. The magic of iron guaranteed supremacy in war.

In the south where the desert stopped at the narrow waterway leading to Arabia and Africa, David wreaked devastation on the Edomites. And when their men lay all dead, he had won a strategic port and a great tract of surrounding land where useful metals filled the dry riverbeds.

In the mountains at the center of David's new kingdom stood the ancient and impregnable walled fortress of Uru-Salim, City of Peace, now called Jebus by its inhabitants. David considered the spot with an intuitive eye. The tribes had settled in such a way that descendants of Leah dwelled south of the city, and descendants of her comatriarch Rachel to the north. The hills round about Uru-Salim were claimed by no one. He knew its traditions of holiness. Jebusites said that the head of Adam the first man was buried near this place. Jews said that their patriarch Abraham had met Melchizedek, Righteous-King, at this place, and that Melchizedek had blessed Abraham with bread and wine even before Abraham had made the covenant of the seed with Jehovah. Canaanites still performed sacred ceremonies in this place, on a circular threshing floor atop a mountain called Zion, the Signpost.

So David took Uru-Salim and made it his own, the City of David, by means of a military maneuver. He penetrated its underground spring. Thousand of years later remnants of David's nation would still pray thanks to Jerusalem for the privilege of using water at night.

For a short time the young house of David, full of devices, fully capable of war, ruled the land from the Orontes River in Syria to the Brook of Egypt. For four hundred miles north to south, and a hundred miles inland from the sea, David's sovereignty sat like a pin connecting the three eastern continents. Settlements flowered in desert, valley, upland. To the southwest in old Cheme, a strip of ancient fertility on the longest river in the world, the old splendor had faded.

Hammurabi was dead in Babylon. The warring kings of Assyria had not yet been born.

When he learned of the capture of Jerusalem—and of the seaport on the southern gulf—King Hiram of Tyre had sent a message of congratulations and friendship to David. This friendship was a boon; Tyre and Sidon and the other Phoenician city-states controlled world trade from India to the Sea of Atlantis. But the island Tyre was incapable of feeding itself, and gladly bought the Hebrews' grain, oil, honey, and wine. In return, the Phoenician king sent David technical advisers in stone, metal, wood, cloth, and dyes.

David also sent Hiram the Transjordanian oak of Bashan for his oars. And Hiram sent the Jews hardwoods from the mountains of Lebanon, out of which the royal city might be constructed.

Soon word of David and his gritty tribes was being carried around the world on Hiram's ships. News of conquests and culture reached the far colonies and trading outposts. Caravans from Egypt and Arabia passing through Israel's toll cities along the Sea Way or the King's Highway picked up information about the monarch and his court and household.

Despite all his bloody battles, David never lost the reputation of a man of love. Passing merchants saw his flame-gold hair, his stature of an angel, and loved him as his people did. They said he played a golden harp, and wrote songs of imperishable beauty. And they renowned the warrior as a hero of the bed. For beautiful David wed or companied with many women, princesses and peasants, foreign and Jewess. From these unions came scores, some said hundreds, of offspring, who shone with the form of David's beauty. His children had long hair, fair and bright, like his, which they wore in pagan fashion in a thick plait from the top of the head. And they rode the golden chariots in the vanguard of the Judaean battle lines.

The traders on their long journeys spoke of these children and of these wives. They liked to talk about the wife Abigail, who had the spirit of a prophetess, and who had come one night on a mule to David's army encampment to plead by her menstrual blood for the life of a man. They gossiped about his

17

cold wife Michal, whose bride-price had been a hundred Philistine foreskins, and who mocked David even so, and gave him no children. It was said Michal fought to have the rights of a man, even to wearing phylacteries. And some whispered that Prince Absalom was not really David's son, but had been foisted upon him by the promiscuous Princess Maacah of Geshur. Certainly it was clear that the sensuous and impulsive Absalom never got along well with his putative father.

But of all David's many women, the most haunting tales were spun about Bathsheba, who bathed before the king. Every detail of their encounter was recreated in the imaginations of men who transported the big larders of honey and grain to lands beyond sea and highway. It was said she told the king her husband Uriah didn't love her. That, indeed, she had only known Uriah a few days before the military zeal of his Hittite upbringing sent him rushing off to fight in the king's army.

When she came into his presence, Bathsheba (it was recounted) noticed how pretty David's eyes were. She was not so beautiful as his wife Abigail. But the shape of her wit and her heart's powers interlocked with the man David's more truly and beautifully. She conceived.

In terror, David called her husband back from the Ammanite battlegrounds, to send him to his wife that he might later think the child in her belly was his own. But Uriah foiled David. He was a commander of a hundred men, and one of the king's thirty best fighters. He protected his soldier's chastity, and slept among the men. David spoke to him; he broached the subject of love and women. But Uriah was firm, austere, and warlike. For a secret moment David and Bathsheba looked at each other, and felt that they were dealing with an alien thing. Then David made his choice.

He sent word to the commander in chief of the Judaean army in siege outside the capital city Amman, in the high mountain gorge where the roads crossed, to put the Hittite in the front line. With the blood of the husband, the city was taken, and its citadel and palace.

There were those who blamed David for this love, saying he had summoned Bathsheba to adultery. And there were partisans of David who asserted that by rights all women in the kingdom belonged to him, and were his trust when he sent their husbands to war.

David considered what he had done, and concluded that he had acted rightly for life. He had made small changes in the quantities of situations, without altering their nature. He had separated a man and wife who did not love, and brought closer a man and woman who did. And he had hastened toward battle a soldier hot for his own valorous death.

The family prophet Nathan did not see it that way, and collected a significant party to condemn. But Nathan was an old man, and long celibate.

The army under David's cousin Joab rejoiced in their victory, and even when the facts surrounding Uriah's death became common knowledge through the machinations of Nathan, these men did not waver in their love for the poet-king. In the palace of the God-King at Amman they found a gold crown as heavy as a man could lift, and they brought it back for David, who cherished it as the only gold he would ever own.

And from the diadem of this crown an incomparable gem was plucked: a great sparkling object with the appearance of the full moon that suddenly fills the skies and speaks in a dream and takes men by surprise and cleaves the soles of their feet to the ground—and this stone was placed into the crown of David. And it contained within it the soul of Solomon. For Solomon was the first surviving child of David and Bathsheba.

THE DEVELOPMENT OF SOLOMON

Solomon was a child of profound passion, and by this he inherited all the tension of the divine coils overhead and beneath our feet. Troubled in his sleep by the accusations of his parents' crimes, he spent the days of his childhood in the royal archives with scribes and lawmen, studying the wisdom of the East. As his father had been a poet and a musician, he became a philosopher and a scientist. And as his father had been a man of war, so he was given to meditation and compromise and called Solomon, the Peaceful, after the city of his birth.

While Solomon was still studying, his world was shaken. Prince Absalom, the most violent of all his many half brothers, ordered the murder of another half brother, the prince Amnon, to revenge Absalom's sister's honor. Civil war broke out, prince against king, with many of David's chiefs on the pretender's side. As the war raged on bitterly, David was forced to flee Jerusalem for his own safety. Later he would return, but in young Solomon's mind crystallized the image of Absalom's entrance into the king's temporarily evacuated capital. For there, swearing by the honor and rights of his sister and his mother, scions of an old, high, royal house, Absalom publicly and with much ceremony went in unto the ten wives of David who were yet inhabiting the city. In a tent spread atop a roof of the king's great house, the prince appropriated his father's harem. Solomon awoke in yet new nightmares, seeing the tent, and Absalom's officiating party, and hearing the awful trumpets. And of the disposition of his father's wives he dared not think.

Later, when his beard had come and he had grown tall, Solomon continued to have unquiet dreams. But they grew colder, and more distant, and drifted like a mist over the wide earth. Chief among them was the dream of Egypt, and the great tetrahedrons. His father the warrior-poet had subjugated the throbbing land, and for the glory of his God had amassed gold and iron. But all the wonders that had been tracked down from abroad or smelted up in the industrial caldrons were as baubles next to the star temples of the old pharaohs. They were said to be immortal, these temples of granite and lime, and to confer immortality on their makers. In Solomon's reveries he heard the schoolmen and the innumerable caravan whispering among the reed and mimosa, telling secrets, as forever above them loomed these marvels of the work of men or genii. He tossed on his straw bed. He let his mind wander in the gate. He schemed to apprehend the method whereby he could equal the achievement of the race that had been the masters of his.

At the age of twenty-one Solomon acceded to the throne. He needed to execute only three persons: his cousin, the leading militarist; his brother, David's oldest surviving son; and the nation's leading scholar, who had favored Absalom. As his first official act, King Solomon contracted with the king of Egypt for a marriage with the royal daughter. Thinking of the might of the late King David who had fashioned metal clothes for his soldiers and expanded the borders of his empire alarmingly, and consulting his diviners for omens, the pharaoh father consented. The dark king of the Great River replied with solemn repressed fury (for no Mistress of the Inscribed House had been sent from Egypt in man's memory) "Let you slay the ass of the covenant between us, my lord, and have peace." As dowry then, Solomon asked for pyramid architects and workmen.

The girl came to meet Solomon at the old high place in Gezer, an Egyptian watchtower town now passing to the Judaeans, and they were wed beside the ten tall standing stones overlooking the sweet lands of Joseph between

Jerusalem and the sea. Then Solomon looked for workmen, and saw instead an array of old men more in need of shrouds than tools. He questioned his bride about architects, and she shrugged.

The new king was at first diverted from his disappointment. For the Egyptian had brought with her, in lieu of a plan for a pyramid, all the different musical instruments known to the times, in gold-trimmed silver, with women to play them, and with each, the story of the god who lived in that sound. For she was herself heir to the age-old Queen of the Thousand Sounds, and had been taught to speak in the many voices of Thebes about the dusk of the Egyptian lily-rose. Beneath a silk canopy jeweled with all the stars in their places, she guided her husband Solomon in his first love, and whispered to him of the meanings of the machines to produce the frequencies.

In his arms the Egyptian said, "I am Nwt, as absolutely naked as the sky, and thou dost hold me to this ground whence I would float in airless bliss, with thy man's right hand upon my loins and thy left hand at my bosom. Thou art a king, my friend! Creative powers support your arms. Beauty reclines at your feet, a drugged, contented servant. Men, a maid, cattle, eight kinds of animal, and two spirits of the afterlife guard our goings out and our comings in. And to each is thought. And to each speech. And in my dream I can hear the music of the gods rising. . . .

tenor panpipe
Adam and Eve

alto panpipe
Osiris the frenetic

skins
Marduk the powerful

six-string lute
Isis in love

horn
Zeus the gregarious

trumpet
Apis the macho

wood flute
Asherah the fertile

silver flute
Lakshmi the ornamented

hammer and strings
Amen the difficult

fifteen-string lute
Radha the mild

double hammer and strings
Thoth the master

low four-string lute
Vishnu the protector

high four-string lute
Jehovah the arrogant." She smiled.

Solomon was happy at first. But his mother, the young widow, took an immediate and intense dislike to his foreign bride. A descendant of kingmakers, she did not conceal her feelings. Indeed, she stormed into the bridal chambers to cut short the honeymoon, claiming the priests required the king on some religious matter. A few days later, Bathsheba gave a speech in court about the attributes of a good woman, with the printed moral that certain persons should not be so considered. The scribes loved it. The new first lady was a sensation.

In a flush of exuberance Solomon worked out an ingenious

trading scheme with his in-laws. Though they were apparently not in the pyramid business anymore, the Egyptians were producing a very efficient and good-looking chariot of wood and iron with gold trim. These the bridegroom negotiated to acquire at a price of four Turkish horses apiece. He stockpiled what he thought he needed for defense. And he resold the rest at a profit to the outlaw Aramaeans in Damascus and to Uriah's people the Hittites.

It was not long, however, before Solomon began to find his wife's ways odd and disconcerting. She made water standing up, and was surprised that he did so. She would not eat for three days around the full moon. When news came of the death of a little brother-cousin in Cheme, she appeared in court with mud on her face and a clutch of bald, barefoot, chanting priests. And she had drawn an unflattering sketch of her mother-in-law on a scrap of red potsherd, under a hieratic curse.

One night Solomon lay awake with his arms around the princess, smelling the scent of henna on her neck. Every week her servants untangled its white flowers from the grapevines where it fed. He considered. He was grateful she had initiated him. Of course there had been that awful scene with his mother. And still Bathsheba and the Egyptian seemed to want to hurt each other. Well, that was no matter. He enjoyed her body. But I don't like her, he thought. In fact he preferred the grape to the henna. She had disappointed him in his main work. She was no scholar: she was vindictive, superstitious, myopic. She thought his big plans as dull as her ancestors'. Like her father and cousins in the Black Land she disdained the monuments of Khufu and Khepere and the house of Mycerinus; she looked back upon the time of the pyramid building as a bad time, a time of irreligion. If there was anything on the plain of Giza she liked, it was only the half-buried lion-human, the sphinx, "the Strangler."

But Solomon's ambition was still unslaked. He understood now that from Egypt would come much silver, but little gold. Their lovemaking through, the king rolled over, to plan. His wife stepped lightly out of bed and retired to her pallet in the finishing room apart. There she smoothed the black stuff around her eyes and the white stuff over her legs with an automatic hand. "Star powders and comet dust," she fantasized. Her imagination was narcotically fluid and never altogether still.

The next morning, in the clear hot sun, Solomon embarked upon a new course of action. There would be a convocation. First he summoned his bodyguard of Cretans and Philistines. Then, with a tumult of scribes and messengers, he convened a cabinet of his appointees: high priest, archdeacon, people's governor, secretary of oxen, raiser of flocks, recorder of transactions, chief of guards, chief of drums and all the music, chief of the coastline, household grand master, wardrobe grand master, chief of horsemen, chief of infantry, standard-bearer, minister of war, jailer, court governor, chief servant, and chief steward.

Then he called a congress of the tribes: the fruitful Ephraimites; the forgetful of Manasseh; the philosophical rapists of Reuben; Gad the robber flocksmen; the vengeful Levites; Asherites and Asheraites from the shore; Simeon bloody with the guilt of slave trade; Issacher the strong ass, the temperate; Zebulon the writer among the ships; Judah of the mountains, called "lion's whelp"; the runner Naphtali; young Benjamin; and the twins Dan and Dinah; these to assemble, swift and righteous, ruler and serpent, soldier and sailor.

And he requested a senate of the men loyal to his brothers, living and dead: to Amnon the eldest, to Absalom the pretender, to Adonijah the anointed. And to Chileab the weak-witted, son of wise Abigail; to the drunken Ithream and to Shephatiah, born in the holy cave at Hebron; and to the many sons of Jerusalem.

Finally he invited the followers of the Hebrew prophetesses: the people of Sarah, and of Miriam who danced around the molten calf, and of Deborah the hornet, called "wife of flame," who held court under a palm tree, and of Hannah who was yet alive and of the Davidic party.

Twenty thousand people answered the king's call, and came together five miles north of the federal city at the high place of Gibeon, where once in the old days the sun had stood still. The king set them to feasting on a thousand oxen ceremoniously slaughtered. Then alone on the eastern hill, Solomon prayed to his God for understanding, and had an auspicious dream that it was granted. He took a haircut. And he presented himself to the gathering with the question of the accomplishment of his mighty ambitions: for himself, for the house of David, for Judah, for all Israel. "How shall we build a temple to the infinite?" he asked them.

In long informal conversations the people who had gathered at Gibeon considered what he had told them, and what they knew of the late king's wishes, and what they wanted on their own account. And they debated the means, and opined, and argued. Friends took one another by the arm and strolled down the long spiral staircase of the old well for refreshment.

Until at last it was decided that Solomon should forthwith ally himself and the nation with Hiram king of Tyre, the best overseer of enterprises known to them in all the lands around.

The Tyrian princess noticed what was happening, and turned away from the admiral. Her father, the architect Hiram, Solomon, and the queen were close together and drinking. She watched the apple in Solomon's great throat jump as the wine went down; she liked his look. Boldly she stepped over to them.

Blurting out the first thing that came to mind, she told the Jew and the Egyptian about the Galli having offered to come in just a moment before their arrival. Solomon nodded politely. He knew the Galli were a touchy internal matter. But the queen was positively disappointed. Memories of childhood in the convent behind the sycamore fig. Nothing more fun than a mad castratus. Oh, bring on the Galli!

Solomon looked quickly back at the man the king had just introduced. In their first glance at each other, at the touch of their hands, the master builder had sensed that it was going to be much better working with King Solomon and King Hiram than it had been to work for Hiram and his father Abibaal. Solomon seemed hopeful, too. He suggested the three of them meet soon in Jerusalem, and this was agreed. The three men smiled at each other warmly.

King Hiram thought: It's a good party.

27

A DANCE

SHEBA WATCHED THE WOMAN DANCING. From her soft seat on the throne, a man-friend's arm lightly around her, the cat black and quiescent at the other side, she could appreciate the finer points of the love dance.

There were many dancers, men and women, and none without grace. But the woman that Sheba was studying had a special grace. The dress she had sewn for herself was a hard white, and the naked flesh that showed of her ribs and arms and neck and ankles (and her thighs, when she moved) was pale and flawless, with the lines of an immature girl's.

But this was no girl.

She moved heavily, stiff-armed and stiff-legged, hardly taking any steps. When the musicians came down on the drum her foot, in a shoe of straw and linen, was in the air. Her narrow rib cage and hips moved only, and these in subtle, tactful movements. She was as if in a sleepwalk, answering only to magnetism: as if a child were stuck in her little birth canal, as if Sheba's entire parade bed throne were lodged inside her to dominate consciousness and slowly, and with infinite dignity, dance out. Her face was refined and proud; she did not forget herself. Now she was edging her way across the field to dance in front of a man who was pretending to see nothing.

He had a hat on, this man. He would be one of the holy. Like many, he was swigging on a waterskin. But like her, he was dancing very quietly, rotating only slightly, and without lifting his feet. His face and body were dark, clean, and noble, and the dancing woman wanted him.

Behind her a high voice sang:

"I want a man for the midsummer revels
Sweet as the boy-god and wise as the sage
True as the lightning
For thus I remember
The elixir of romance that spurns the grave."

The circle of flames throbbed hypnotically, and the long strings boomed in the blood. Under a tamarind tree far off Sheba saw a slim young man lingering to watch her on her throne; that was good. She wished to dance. But it was dangerous for a monarch. She looked one more time at the dancers.

Then the queen set aside the lion skin and rose. The little cat jumped down from his soft seat and ran into the crowd. The man with the hat was imperceptibly rejecting the dancer in white. He was free. Sheba walked away from the dance, brushing the arms of men with the tip of her finger as she passed them. Their charges ran through her.

 A DAM

THE COMPANY AT ABIBAAL'S WAS BREAK-
ing up into small groups. The architect had excused himself
from the kings, their business transacted, in order to return to
his work on the new Melkarth pavilion for the mainland. King
Hiram was leading King Solomon over to the technocrats to
hear about a certain impressive structure in the south. In a
cluster near the musicians, the Yemenite hydraulics minister
was explaining the dam of Marib to the Persian agronomist and
several others. Nearly everyone in the room (with the possible
exception of the Egyptian lady) had an obsessive interest in
water.

The hydraulics minister was short and neatly dressed. Over a
plain shirt and knotted skirt, his dark coat was hidden beneath
wide crisscrossed belts studded with jewels. Into these were
stuck a canteen and a large curved knife, on which his hand
lightly rested. His eyes were burning earnest, his nose small
and rounded, and a mustache made a fine line over his full lips.

"Then suddenly the sky darkens," he was saying, "and there
come the flood rains—!" On the word "rains" he suddenly
drew the knife from its silver sheath and cut a swath through
the air in front of him. The Persian leaned warily away.

"But you understand what these sudden, brutal rains mean
to us?" he continued, showing a row of perfect white teeth.
The Persian was nodding, but the Yemenite went on. "You

have canals from your rivers. We have nothing like that. Only parching dryness and the downpour!"

"Of course, we focus mainly on the Tigris," said the agronomist, who had a full beard, a long all-white turban, and a sad look in his eyes. "This dam of yours took a long while to build, hmm?"

"By Ilumquh! Two hundred years!" said the hydraulics minister, with a noticeable licking of the lips. His knife slowly found its way back into the sheaf in his belt. "And we never would have done it," he said, leaning close into the face of the man from the Tigris, "if it hadn't been for—"

Just then Kings Hiram and Solomon interrupted the conversation. A glimmer of interest in Solomon's face was more than mere politeness. He had caught some of the minister's words. Hiram introduced him to his guests and prompted them to describe the dam, and how it worked. The belted man complied willingly, outlining the process of collecting the only water to be had in southern Arabia. How there were no rivers, and no regular rains. How for a few weeks a year the floods poured from the sky, in their own time, and these his people collected in a reservoir high above their fields. How slowly, with measure and order, through the sluice gates and aqueducts and large canals and small canals, the land became fertile.

Solomon was thinking about the minister's earlier remark. Two hundred years. A spring of imperialist envy had been tapped. He burst in with questions. Who was the architect of the dam? Where was the work force drawn from? How were they organized? How was their morale? How much were they paid?

The hydraulics minister welcomed the king's questions so keenly he grabbed the shy young monarch and practically embraced him. He described for Solomon the barrenness of the land before the coming of the Sabaeans, and exuberantly praised the virtues of the queens whose lifework it had been to contribute to the building of the great system, and not to see its completion. He recited wage and price statistics.

A forlorn smile came across the face of the Persian agronomist. He looked expectantly at Solomon, but the king was withholding his reaction. His lips were pursed, and he had a preoccupied air. He drew back. His wife, he noticed, was flirting with the admiral. Not surprising.

"Queens, you say."

"Highness?"

"You say you had queens over you for two hundred years?"

The minister looked at the king intensely. "And we still do."

The image of woman that occurred to Solomon at that moment was his mother's. Her naked limbs dripping from the bath, seen from the Tower of David. The only blot on his godly father's armor . . .

The minister studied Solomon's silent brow.

Then Solomon remembered his wife. A doll, a toy.

"How do women wage war for you?" he demanded of the Sabaean.

The armed man's eyes grew black and large. "We have known peace for five hundred years."

Now Solomon really was startled. In his very name was his family's wish for peace. And the only great peace in his memory was the peace in Egypt when his race had been slaves to . . . hers. In discomfort he looked at the pharaoh's daughter in the corner laughing and shaking her ringed fingers at the admiral. He collected himself. He bade the minister elaborate. To what did he attribute the peace?

The hydraulics minister was eloquent. "It is our great good fortune," he said, "to possess gems and metals in abundance, as well as many animals, fruits, and foodstuffs. Our estates and meadowlands and orchards are so rich that falling fruit blocks the road and fills baskets left unattended. Abundance keeps our towns safe from robbers and wolves. Even the bath stoker wears a golden belt.

"In the section where I live there grow in addition a variety of spiritual plants. There are some whose burning is desired by worshipers around the world." The minister indicated a small dish near the musicians' dais, from which spiraled up a light, fragrant smoke. "In Canaan it is not so common. But in some places our camels go—China, I might mention—one finds whole families of persons conditioned from birth to be smokers and smoke swingers. And many lives centered around a product only we can provide."

33

"This has made you wealthy?" said Solomon. The minister nodded.

"And the empire of Sheba, with all its wealth, is isolated, surrounded on all sides by impenetrable boundaries: ocean, desert, the harshest cliffs."

Solomon urged the minister to delineate the boundaries of Sheba.

And the dark-skinned Yemenite waxed lovingly on the description of his native queendom. Some of what he said could have been verified—such as that his people's capital cities clustered together along both shores of the Red Sea at that precise point where a great landmass stretches off to the easterly and another, even greater, stretches to the westerly, and they meet, close as a kiss. And some other of his contentions were like seeds on the wind, only by chance to take root in a credulous, yearning substratum of Solomon's brain— claims made smilingly, as if magically to expedite their acceptance—that the trees which grew in this land were offshoots from the trees of Eden, that the waters were sweet and the dust of the ground like gold dust, that happiness showed on the brows of the people like a wreath. . . .

"I would like to meet your queen," murmured Solomon, with a lust for body or power or wisdom it could not be determined.

BOOK THE SECOND

FROM THE POINT
OF VIEW OF SHEBA

THE QUEENDOM

Years and years ago when Africa was a network of loosely connected nations ruled by women and the Trojan War was past but Homer not yet born, there lived in Sheba a queen. Though Solomon in Jerusalem was wiser than all the children of the East, and of Egypt, the queen of the south was very possibly wiser. Wisdom permeated her, and made her beautiful. On account of this her fame was great, from the jungles of Shaba in the west to the high dam of Sabaea in the east, throughout Ethiop and down past the elliptical fortress of the Zimbabwe. One time a splendid hunter-king of China traveled six thousand miles to see her and converse with her in garden and bower.

The queendom of Sheba rolled out lavishly, over mountains and plateaux, across many good rivers and growing land, from the places where day and night were always most equal, to the deep narrow holes in the ground into which, since time long gone, women and men had climbed to pull out the soft, shiny, yellow metal. Bouncing off the edge of great Egypt, Sheba slung softly down the belly and uterus of Ophir, past the Nilotic cradle and the great rift and on to the farther cape.

In this wide expanse love was law, more powerful than man. The smell of love (not mutilation and frenzy, as it had become in some places, but mellow love and rich) slipped through the northeast corridor, through the oases, blending easily with the ways of Dravidia and losing itself on a peak in the Himalayas.

Love swung back down, from the olive and coffee skins of the Hindus and Semites to the bright copper faces at the Red Sea, and expired in bliss in the ebony buttered flesh of the Hamites, their cousins. In Sheba, long-haired men, pleasant and strong, the tallest on the earth, loved women who were in all things their sisters. Nakedly thin, their plain white robes left them uncushioned on the edge of experience. For recreation of nerves they smoked qat and cannabis, and drank beer. They were bred to love; they were well-bonded. In Sheban night, lean burnished body strained and pulsated and turned to merge and meet, enfold surround, another body long and slender.

The Shebans loved each other in a kind of unison that would later be forgotten. When the ibex horns of the new moon appeared each time in a sky thick with fat stars, the women of the queen bled. And when the moon was full again the women knew they were fertile, and conceived. Twelve groups of children were born each year, each one dreamed of on a full-moon night. And of all the children the happiest and the most lissome were the children of the midsummer moon, who took breath at the equinox of spring. For this was Sheba's only religion: that in hut and tent, under baobab, mahogany, or palm bough, it was good that man and woman be together when the round white moon hung heavy in the lap of the hottest sun.

Thus they were, so many millennia ago, in a morning of dew and mist.

Beneath the blinding rays of the sun she lay in silent, motionless ecstasy. It was the custom daily to do homage to the yellow ball and to greet the warmth and the light with prostrations. She dreamed. "Dependent on the sun, all will indeed divide the storm wealth among the born and the yet to be born, with vigor." Sheba counted her wealth in trees, stones, and waters. The queen of the south knew the ancestral properties of wood, herb, perfume, medicine and spice. She understood jewel and gem. In intuitive sympathy with the waters that raged beneath the crust of the world and ebbed and flowed with the celestial tides, she reckoned the basic stuff of reality as passion. Her people wrote their names on rock, and the names of their lovers in the trees. And they watched the trees change and grow and finally die, and did not mourn.

One day a shiver interrupted Sheba at her sun morning adorations and caused her to open her brown eyes and look up. She had imagined that the sun was blocked to darkness for an instant by the wings of a bird wearing a golden crown. She saw men feasting in a kingdom to the north. She saw a man with a crown looking around, looking for her.

Later that same day a merchant party arrived in Axum by way of Marib, carrying red copperglass and wine, forks and safety pins. A king called Solomon, said the fleetmaster Tamrin to the palace people, was asking for gold, ivory, and blue sapphires to be used in a major building project in Jerusalem—and offering to pay double their worth. He had reportedly also expressed an interest in frankincense.

In the curved walls of the queen's harem there were many false windows. Only a few gave out onto the open sky. An old woman was uncovering some of these now with slow and bending arms. Outside the air was clear, with just a shadow of gray in the clouds that made it seem all the more clear.

The silk robe of Mu Wang rustled smoothly along the shiny black floors.

Little Brother, the princess, was throwing a golden ball into the air and catching it, laughing and squealing, "Look at me!" Sheba did not stop for her, nor did she give her a thought. The queen stepped over the threshold of an oval room dappled with light. The library. All the books women had ever written were piled and stacked precariously on the shelves here: reed and papyrus rolls in urns, animal and goatskins on wood, clay paintings, and stone carvings that went back nine or ten millennia. The librarian was sucking drowsily on a smallish antler. To this woman Sheba addressed herself.

"Who is this man Solomon?"

The librarian was an ancient soul, a hundred or two hundred years old (it was said), with a concise body and a vision behind heavy eyelids that could cut a line in glass. She slept under an aloe inside the library and approved of and appreciated everything that ever was or ever would be—with the exception of the big-breasted pythoness, whom she hated.

"Solomon is a magician-king," she replied without opening her eyes.

"Does he challenge me?" asked Sheba. "Is there something I should fear?"

"There is much said and much written about this Solomon," replied the old woman, pulling out a heavy book from a shelf behind the aloe and rocking back and forth very slightly. The archivist was nothing if not aware of the sides of arguments; in this she was very different from the pythoness, who liked to make a simple point, even if it were wrong. Both had their followers. At length she put her pipe down on a branch of the tree and opened her eyes to look at Sheba.

"All right," she said. "Behind the magic there are four real power sources for you to watch." Sheba rested her chin in her hand. "One. Iron chariots. Which he doesn't use. Two. Trade routes. Which you can negotiate. . . ." She paused. "The other two are trickier."

Sheba leaned forward, and commanded her brain to open and hear entirely; and the librarian triggered her own cavernous memory to yield up and feed to her tongue correctly what she once knew and would recreate.

"First of all, the flying carpet. My book tells me Solomon moves about on a rug that birds pull through the air so it seems to be flying. Now we know this is beyond our technology.

"But there may be a problem in translation." Translation was a favorite subject of the old one. "What do the Syrians mean by 'bird'? Upon close reading of many shards I believe they mean 'spirit hungry for truth.' And the 'rug' may indicate some kind of rapt state, or perhaps festivity. Then the story of many birds all towing one rug would mean something about the unified force of plural spirits, especially as they seem in festivity or trance.

"Be that as it may, the flying carpet story has an important point for us. It has been said that one time Solomon was flying about on his carpet, for his own magical purposes, when one of the bird crew—the one with a golden crown on its head—moved out of place and let the sun shine down on him."

Something thumped in Sheba's chest. She suppressed an impulse to speak.

"To make a long legend short, Solomon was going to kill the bird when it finally returned much later, but the bird told him it had gone looking for water, and that it had found the waters of creation, the holy fire, paradise itself. Do you know what it was talking about?"

"Yes," said Sheba, "it was talking about us."

"Correct," said the librarian. "Solomon's emissary spirit found us."

"Is that bad?" The queen of Sheba was resting her chin now on the opposite hand and elbow.

The librarian picked up her antler pipe, stoked it with a finger, and took a puff. "I'd feel a little better about it," she said, "if Solomon referred to us as something other than 'the land of incense.' I think that way of putting it suggests a mistake in orientation."

"Well, what shall I call him?"

As the librarian smiled, long archaic splay rayed out from her eyes and framed her coldly compassionate mouth. "Good question," she said. She thought a minute. Then: *"Suleïmân* will throw him off."

There followed a long contented silence. The librarian's eyelids drifted downward. Sheba worried that she'd go to sleep. "You mentioned one other thing—" she said.

"Oh, yes," answered the librarian, alert enough. "The calendar. But I wouldn't worry about that. It's not important."

"Don't worry about what?"

"Well, if you must . . ." From a knot in the tree, the old librarian fetched out a goblet made of a single transparent green stone, and took a long drink from it. She wiped her mouth carefully and sighed.

"It seems," she said, "that in the early days of this magician-king's suzerainty he was informed that the moon calendar was not lining up right with the sun. Each year the planting month was inching deeper and deeper into the cold season. So this Solomon called a small court or council or lodge of six men and himself to handle the difficulty.

"And these men whom he called together were Benaiah (Son of Ia), Joseph ben Barakhya (Son of Lightning), Ahiah (Brother of Ia), Ahishar (Gate of My Brother), Elihoreph (Judge's

41

Pause), and Remirat. Remirat's name seems to mean Decay of Women, but perhaps that's wrong. By profession these six were a military man (later to become head of the council of seventy), a secretary and two scribes, the head of Solomon's household, and . . . well, there's Remirat again. For occupation we have listed only: demon.

"When they were done, they had added an extra moon-month seven times every nineteen years, and I understand the seasons work out all right like that. But that's not important.

"What was important was that they called what they had done—and broadcast it, and made sure all the scribes spelled it correctly—'the secret of timing.' Now, what did the phrase 'the secret of timing' mean in Syria? Simply this. It meant the work the women had always done to estimate when they might become pregnant. For, you know, they are all irregular there.

"So," smiled the librarian, "that's all. Do you understand?"

Sheba rent the pocket of the Chinese king's silk robe. She turned and fled the library, and went out among the woods and stones of the forest to seek the place of the snake and the woman who kept them.

In shrines where the python presided, women with long calloused arms partook of the sacrament of the snakebite. From the times of the caves till long after the first cuttings of agriculture the ritual had been thus: ecstasy and prophecy following upon the kiss of krait and cobra. The immunity of long practice. The pythoness in transport vocalized a past, present, and future that were concentric. The word was not yet as holy as the sound, and so the women of the snake expressed what was revealed to them in song and chant, in pitch, rhythm, and tone. And there were no orthographers.

The big-bellied, big-breasted snake woman met the queen at the door and kissed her and took her in. A heavy cobra lay immobile on the floor.

"Tell me about the sky time lore, Mama," said the queen of Sheba, "and whether women invented it, and whether men stole it."

The pythoness laughed very, very deeply in her stomach, and almost silently. Then, to warm herself up for the reception of the muse, she chanted in a low and rumbling voice: "I am a

42

Janjera. I eat ensete. I use the hoe. I live at the Great Divide, where the earth was rent and women came out to make life. My hut is on Mount Bor, where the giant snake lives who made the world, who now only shudders in anger. Not far away are the startings of seven rivers. You know one of my rivers. You call it the longest river on the earth. I know you. I call you human sacrifice."

Then she stopped. Inhabiting no place. She rolled her eyes beyond seeing and let the lids float and took a breath in meditation on how-to-up-for-at-with, and in a different, higher, dusty voice, she uttered her answer to Sheba's question: "The red moon, maker of the month, indeed, saw the stars going along the route. Having observed she rises up like a carpenter with a bent back: be witness of this, O heaven and earth."

It was sufficient. Sheba determined to be brave, to take steps.

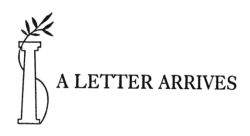

A LETTER ARRIVES

TWO THOUSAND MILES AWAY SOLOMON was sitting on the steps of the brazen altar eating some lamb. Shame of Bathsheba ran in his blood, and greed of the Druids' tin and the Edomites' copper, and the thrill of the golden chariots, and the pure breath of science won out of Philistia's ironworks in a moment of wit.

A bit of fat dripped into his beard. Quickly he brushed away the offending smudge and murmured the charm against fever. By the throne of the most high God he commanded the demon germ which is in dirt to retreat from the creature divinely fashioned.

Then the king rose and walked through the motionless Levantine afternoon to his chambers. Twenty unfinished parchment manuscripts were crowded on a low table there. Solomon employed three scribes to help him: the Jews Elihoreph and Ahiah, and the Arab ben Barakhya who was his chief secretary, as Solomon himself had been to his father. Like his father, he worked without allowing himself so much as an afternoon of idleness, for he had much to complete. In stolen moments the three scribes trained a school of Solomon to continue the work after their master's death.

And these are the writings of Solomon that have come down:

Three Thousand Proverbs
A Thousand and Five Songs

45

The Song of Songs, Which Is Solomon's
The Book of the Acts of Solomon
History of the Wonders of the World
The Book of Medicaments
The Book of Secrets
The Seal
On the Choice of Attributes
The Upper Mirrors
The Work of the Judges
The Book of Hiding Places
The Book of Experiments
The Book of Age
The Book of Parables
The Book of Perfection
The Book of Works
The Book of Unity
The Book of Study
The Book of Observance of Customs
The Book of the Will
The Book of Honesty
The Book of Prayer
The Book of Faith
The Book of Choice
The Book of Inspiration
The Book of Promptness
The Book of the Sects of Wise Men
The Book of the End of All Things
Measurement
Speculations on the Metals
The Four Letter Name
The Seven Sky Lamps
A Treatise on Colors
The Book of the Seasons
On the Nine Candles
On the Tribes

A letter arrived. Attendants wanted to rush it into the library urns for storage, but first Sheba turned it over and over to hear the message in its words. Its paper was a washed palm leaf, its ink an aromatic glittering mixture of black amber, saffron, and gold. Its alphabet was the snakes frozen and fossilized on a page. Later the librarian would identify the dragon-fierce script as Syriac, and guess that Solomon himself had invented this variant.

Sheba, still perusing, was more at home with the international language of picture signs, name marks, symbols. The name of neighboring Egypt, inside a curved-corner frame, was not to be seen. That was a relief. Nor was there the sign of the Big Medicine of Umhlopegazi inside a double axhead. That was well, too. But wait. With goods imported by Tamrin from the north had appeared the six-sided insignia of one of those kings and, even more recently, the top-up five-sided sign of this rascal Solomon. Now here was Solomon's seal again, on a missive direct to her, inside a circle, and with the royal flower in the center.

That evening it took Sheba and her first minister some hours of pondering, a burst of inspiration, and the librarian's drowsy advice, to unravel the rest of the message as follows: I SOLOMON SON OF DAVID KING OF ISRAEL BID THEE O ANCIENT KING SAYING HASTEN FORTHWITH AND COME UNTO ME.

"What does it mean?" said Sheba.

"It means, 'Come before me, thou and thine, and salute me, and I will honor thee above all my kings,'" said the librarian.

"It means, 'If you come not before me I will choke you and your captains in your beds and bedchambers and devour the flesh from your bones and destroy your cities,'" suggested the first minister.

The queen and the first minister walked together along the paths in the moonlight. From out of the star-cloud, Antares Oldest Ear Jewel sparkled red and green. A light drizzle brought the peacocks to the roofs to dance. The message had come not only by courier but also by bird wing, gossip, and rumor, the self-interested tales of merchants. Solomon and his scribes were undeniably powerful controllers of the media. The queen of Sheba thought of him and she felt a *frisson*. She lusted to meet him. It would seem he was equally impatient to meet her.

Although Sheba had loved a thousand men, in the way of the

47

queens of Sheba, she was fresh as a virgin. And this was in part due to the arts of the woman beside her, her first minister and priestess of opiates.

The woman walking with the queen had grown up close by. The business of their childhoods had been seen to by the same intimate companionate. But at an early age the minister, and not the other, had lost trust. Pictures of a man striking a woman, of a small baby dying, hung in her memory. She never spoke of them, but her mind silently took on their fierce colors. She mastered many crafts. She healed or distracted many with her arts. But though she laid her head down on the grass with hope in her eyes, and the white pinfeathers of the ostrich in her long ears, she found in love again and again only the violence and desertion she expected of it. She was a little shorter than the queen.

The two reentered the harem and sat long hours into the night discussing Solomon. Over tendrils of resinous smoke and plates of game and white salt cheese they discussed whether it was wise to pursue this northern king and search out his heart. There were bound to be problems. To start with, three million men and women thought the queen of Sheba was the most wonderful human being on the planet; Solomon was very likely to see this as a threat. His countermeasures in the way of defense might hurt. A long foreplay with a rough character was probably inevitable. And afterward? There was no saying.

"He'll rape you," said the minister with alacrity.

"I'll ask him in the beginning not to."

At which the young minister leaned forward and whispered, "They breed for size in the north. The men are big. The women are smaller."

"Mother of work!" exclaimed the queen. "That's serious."

Sheba set her pipe down and began to toy with the meat, pushing it back on the dish with the long finger of her left hand. She knew, in a wordless way, that the goddesses and gods spoke to their subjects differently, and echoed differently in their heads by day, and gave them different dreams at night. But if the women of the father-god rewarded the bigger men with their love and bore to them, the whole balance of power in the world might be shifted.

"On the other hand," said the queen, and paused. She mused to herself about halves and sides and inheritances and truth. Her wisdom implied a longing for truth as the sun implies radiance, and she longed to watch the truth circling out from the lips of the wisest man on earth. By coincidence or providence, Solomon, the magician-king, was there for her, in her time. It was her feeling to go, she said at last. She joked: "I want a man with an earring; I will slip it off when we make love and hide it under my mat, and he shall know that he has been had by me."

The minister cocked her head to one side. She knew Maqda to be a very straight-ahead person; she must find out, she must know. Herself, she was more dubious in all things, and took cover under what might be called dishonesty. A trip by the queen to see King Solomon sounded like some kind of capitulation to her. But she understood the nature of choices, and how one is alone in them.

"I'll go with you," she said.

At this moment Tamrin entered noisily through a curtain of shells. He was a humorous, energetic man, of Yemenite, Chaldean, and, it was rumored, Phoenician descent. By trade he plied the foreign markets in ships, for goods to sell to the women of Sheba. And when he was in Axum he entertained the queen with gifts and chatter.

The first minister rose and left. She couldn't stand the fellow. She ran her hand along the wall.

Tamrin was full of stories of Solomon. He took credit for introducing the subject in Sheba. It made him feel he had a bet on a strong horse. There was fresh news in the seaport cities. . . .

Sheba was not listening to him so much as watching the bobbings of his head. In a new side of the queen's brain was enciphering a letter of reply to the Hebrew filiarch. Her language would be southern, her letters those of the northern soothsayers. A shepherd would conceal the token in his staff and deliver the message overland by night.

"I shall come."

Now she began to pay attention. Tamrin was saying that Solomon had sent a whole armada of Phoenician sailors up sea toward the ports of Sheba, with the intention of selling products for gold. When he saw that she had started listening, he threw her a new trinket from the north.

"What's this little arab?"

It was a mirror of green Phoenician ironglass. Sheba looked down her small straight nose at the reflection: at the lines of her calm wide eyebrows, at the tight black cap of hair that spilled out in a waterfall below the crown. Reflexively she smiled at both sides of her face.

"I've decided to go to Jerusalem," she told the merchant. Tamrin's reaction to this news was so boisterous that the queen deliberately set the mirror down next to some Egyptian ointment jars he'd brought her that she'd never used. She often disagreed with the man's taste. But he was very concrete, and often useful. "Brief me on their civilization."

So Tamrin told Sheba all he knew: what kinds of things the people in the north wore and ate and manufactured for themselves and manufactured for barter; and when he was done, Sheba didn't know any more than she had learned from the librarian. He suggested that she wear trousers on the journey there, and, once in Solomon's court, trade off among Arabian cloak and boot, Abyssinian three-piece with apron, Egyptian bodice gown, and long skirt of Ophir.

"I didn't ask what I should wear," said Sheba mildly. "In my treasury are vats of gold dust, pots of emeralds, urns of sapphires blue and red, chests of pearls. It is these Solomon will see, not my rags." The Sheban's figure was airy and exercised, and she wore all the different kinds of costumes as were worn throughout her empire. "I might, like a friend, like a sister, sprinkle the precious dust and gems in benediction. Or, again, I might heave a priceless rock at the king.

"That's what I'm curious about," said Sheba. "Is it to be war or peace?"

The ways of the queen's civilization had been perfected over aeons. They had no bows and arrows; they did not fight man against man. At the edges of their round homes they hunted the beast with axes and clubs; but even this, they sensed, had not always been so. Mother and grandmother passed down the story that in the dawn of beginnings leopard and deer had lain down beside one another and been friends, and all families had

50

eaten abundantly of the blue-green grain. It seemed that the civilizations of the north were different. Like filings to a moving coil Sheba was drawn to the vortex of the new power.

Tamrin had no answer for her. The terms of the encounter were wholly new.

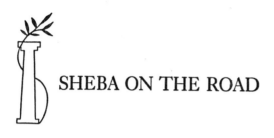

SHEBA ON THE ROAD

Out of the high plateaux of uncon-quered Abyssinia, she came by the sea. In a fleet of seventy-five boats curved like the new moon, spoon-ruddered to the length of four men, guarded with long spears, she arrived in beauty and majesty at Solomon's provincial Gulf harbor. Eyewitnesses were dazzled and unreliable. The local governor was over-whelmed. "And have you come by the waters or the heavens?" he said in wide-eyed welcome. And, "Do you walk with God?" And, "The whole world is under your sandals. We worship your breath."

Thence she rode on a white camel of prodigious size and exquisite poise past the black goat-hair tents of the bedouins, where little boys came running and stared up in amazement at the line she made. Around her swayed giraffes that had been transported by way of the west, and hippopotami. Six hundred camels in her entourage each held nearly five hundred pounds of goods. Fifty elephants followed; four royal Numidian lions; uncountable mules.

In the camels' heavy waterskin sacks were pots of the gum of the frankincense tree. Myrrh leaves and its red resin. Gold. Pink pearls from the sea of reeds. Ivory tusks. Nard and ambergris. The black resin of rockrose. Moon coriander. Myrtle and oliban. The endangered storax. Hops.

Sheba passed an old high place that had recently gone from Egyptian into Judaean hands. She was wearing the trousers of the horse riders of the north and reclining in a peacock-feather litter munching a cake of blue teff, while beside her slept a cat in a black and white wig.

Outside the city of seven wells a noble from the Jerusalem court appeared with an advance party. He strode like a warrior, solid and mature, but with a gentleness also. Sheba thought it might be Solomon himself, and descended from the howdah. The Israelite laughed; it was only Son of Ia. But he was a gallant intermediary, sent because it was said of him that he could charm the milk away from a lioness. The queen invited him atop the great beast with her, and, empathetically, the two parties merged.

Listen to the music Solomon heard as Sheba's train raised up dust in the distant desert. Smell the scents too sweet for him to describe. The smoke of her incense rose above the caravan like a phallus, and told him that she brought herbs, the white powder, all the spice stuffs of the merchants.

I am Sheba. My right ankle is scarred where the Monomatapa hacked at it one time because I danced too well in public. But my legs are strong as fire in despite of this, and in my dreams I still dance; I fly with the three priestesses; I ride in the golden car drawn by day and night. In the flood season I like to walk through the waving grainfields below the dam, and to sit and think on the ridge of black rock north of Marib. When I go back to Ophir across the Gate of the Weeping, my friends meet me with the throne.

Officially I am a virgin, else I could not be queen. But in truth I have had many men. My people understand the power of love, and they love me—the companions of my youth who braid my hair and listen to me with affection and tolerance, and the boys and men who have been to my bed and do not trouble the secret.

Some say I killed a man for the throne. It is not so. On the west shore they name the man I killed Arwe, and on the east coast they name him "the Tobba." And in both places they say he ruled for four hundred years and ate virgins. I promulgated a social reform, is all: I stopped them from putting little girls in with the snakes. The xalkydra doesn't need little girls. It can make do with a goat, or an old woman who's become immune. Perhaps I attained a modest fame for that.

In eastern Sheba, the land of the dam, the first ruler of the nomads was called Sun Mother, and Saba, the Captor. She was kin to The Small. And she began the great hydraulic work, and the setting of the cities, with the help of her librarian and scribe Lokman. After her there were some among the queens my mothers who kept their consorts as virtual prisoners, but that time has passed.

I had always believed that I was descended from these distant cousins of the nomad people. But when the Chinese king came to visit, he told me a long elaborate story—in that very polite way I have come to think of as Chinese—about how I was known in his country. Yes, they had heard of me in the Middle Kingdom. I'm not sure why: perhaps for the snake reform or, more likely, the herb and resin trade. They said there that I was the daughter of a Chinese king and a fairy. That my mother had thrown my older brother into the flames. And that, despite my father's initial horror, she had vindicated herself by leading him to a military victory. Strange story. But they may be right.

We smoked some yarrow together, and he went away much moved.

Long ago the Sabaeans crossed the watery gate into Ophir and mixed with the darker woman tribes. I was born in Ophir and raised and educated among the women in the sleeping gardens of Ethiopia, where the roses have sixty petals and the lemons are sweet. All the rooms in our sanctuary opened onto the gardens. We sat under the trees and ate cress and listened to the tales of travelers returning from the lower Nile or the lands of the ax. The afternoon I heard an old crone from the storytellers' guild speak about the great pyramids, I remember I was watching a yellow butterfly playing near a plane tree.

I was kept pure, in my childhood, for I was born to be priestess or queen. I drank no beer and ate no meat, and neither touched nor saw any frightening thing. I was taught by old women and holy men, now Brahmanas, now Pygmies, now the tall Watusi, about the ways of my land, and the hieroglyphics we play with, and how to cherish the sacred library and respect the librarian. I came to know that we are a people, a family, a nestling of clans, and that the pulse of life beats hard in us. We propagate. We live by the dream voices. The tastes of the earth are sweet on our tongues. The child in the heart is satisfied, and does not grow old. I came to know that our place is called on the outside Saba, or Sheba, which means man, or woman's part, or merchant, or old one. But we care nothing for these names. The names come from the thundering cities of On and Babylon, where sticky asphalt disguises great gaping holes in the ground, and men and women live in dizzy towers, and the tension in the head overtakes and silences the beating of the blood. Still, though I do not welcome it, I know that we will in the end be sucked up and eaten by the cities. A babe will be born who, in mistaken innocence, will lead us there.

When the first red moon came, I was asked to choose between the world of immaterial beings and that of humans. How does one make such a decision? I read the writings on the harem wall; the marvelous funny inscriptions that run right, and then left, and then right, and then left again. I listened to the voices of the woods and the ocean. I sat very still on the cliffs. I decided to live by the light of love. I traveled to see him who admits to no bodily imperfections, the Monomatapa of Zimbabwe, and that one took me in the dance and made the sacrificial cut. Thus I became a human.

And thus I was proclaimed queen, and my good friend from childhood my first minister. We decided that she would fulfill the mystery functions, and I the mundane. Sometimes queens had really gone wrong trying to handle both. But I found that there was not that much for me to do. Justice prevailed the length and breadth of my large and flourishing empire.

I thought frankly that we were rich enough. We sent our herbs and resins overland by mule to a great many different places. They were light enough to carry, and drew a high price in silver and gold. And since our traders had no particular interest in buying the products of other places, they returned with the metals. Our goldsmiths and silversmiths perfected their crafts. Then Tamrin and his tribe tamed the camel for me, and our overseas trade exploded overnight. The camel could cross desert and silt on his big, padded feet, and did not require to be watered. Our caravans reached China.

Now I suppose we are the richest people in the world. And this despite—or because—we are not greedy; we do not feel that another man's wealth is our opportunity. The money for our plants piles up. We drink from goblets of every description. Our furniture stands on silver feet. Our walls are leaf gold. Our ceilings and doors are ivory, and jewels are everywhere. Well, there's no end to it.

Tamrin is a talented man, though occasionally irritating. I had to reward him for his services. I made him fleetmaster. He enjoys the travel.

So Sheba is in touch with all the cities of the world, and I find myself part of this great whirlwind of trade. I have come a long way in my life, from the purity of the sleeping gardens to this rock-strewn road, going toward a pile of iron. If it were not for the man Solomon, I would not be doing it. There is nothing more important than a person.

We have a saying in Sheba, "I want a man for the midsummer revels: sweet as the boy-god and wise as the sage . . ." and so on. I was thinking, What men have I known? Who was sweet as the boy-god? And I thought: Lijj. So gravely sweet. So young! The face and body of a spirit. He listened to me, with thoughtful impatience, and went on away again after his own soul.

But who was wise? I heard myself thinking. Whose wisdom can I stand under the banner of my beauty? What man has wisdom for Sheba the queen to hear? Whose armed mind will be my ideal in a long winter speculating toward the heat? Does such a one exist?

And then came word of Solomon, whom the six winds call wise.

I know he is wealthy. Tamrin says he trades the horses and hemp of Turkey for the metal cars of Egypt and sells both, after his commission, to the kings of the Aryans who use them to promote the fortunes of their war gods. Is this wise?

I shall test his famous wisdom. My questions will be hard and difficult to speak about. I shall ask him of politics, of sex, and of science. I will find out whether the wisdom of his old hermit god is superior to that of my fat mother.

Maid! Bring us jujubes and whey! What does Solomon eat? Meat, I have heard. What is that you say?—nothing but unmixed barley bread, in fear of poisons? But you joke.

The journey is hot. Before you came I enjoyed the talk of the camelmen and the commotion at the toll cities. I polished my riddles as I dozed. I intended to know whether Solomon's wit be real or only imagined by the propagandists, worldly or only local color.

Most important, I shall ask him to explain to me in his man's words the significances of the tide phases, and how they conjunct on the great year. Does he hear the waters churning to the shores, and the life in the core of woman, and does he provide for her? Or does he want only to prong and slay?

O God and her consort, help me! I fear in my thighs that life as I have known it is doomed! My foremothers fought under Memnon alongside the Amazons to defend Helen's throne, and lost. The fire in Troy! And Hit! And Sumer, where Inanni was murdered! The scribes and minstrels of all the earth are kept busy trying to apprehend the projections of these turbulent politics!

I understand that there are many lands of my sisters and lovers that will not be remembered. Their clans will die and still there will be boys in cities who will know Solomon. They will have forgotten the names of Lycia, and Ogygia, and Cantabri, and Lelege, and Caria, and Aetolia, and Pelasgia, and Catal Huyuk, and Caucone, and Erech, and Arcadie, and Epeia, and Tel-Halaf, and Minua, and Teleboia, and Sheba. Sheba will be forgotten. For this I grieve.

"What use to visit the enemy in his camp?" my people wondered, with justification. The faces of my friends showed sad bitter pride. They gave me a subdued warning, and let me go.

But I had to come. I had to make this trip. Something determines my path, beyond even choosing. Don't say that I admire or envy Solomon in Jerusalem. Say that I feel him a worthy adversary. Something will happen between us. I am willing to risk it.

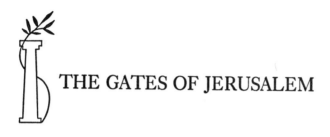

THE GATES OF JERUSALEM

JERUSALEM SAT ATOP ONE OF A GROUP OF several rolling hills whose valleys curved gently around the summit. In the stony plains below it was hot, but as the caravan passed upward the air grew suddenly cooler. Along both sides of the city road, leaves of the low olive trees glinted silver in the sun.

Gray buildings of the capital city outcropped: the baking house on the left, royal gold dust in a warehouse at the right. The olive orchards gave way to vineyards, guarded over by lanky watchmen. And then, as suddenly as the air had changed, huge squared rock gates suddenly appeared above and ahead of the travelers, framed by orchards of fig and quince, wild cinnamon trees, the stepped terraces of sandalwood. Here a kitchen garden of a merchant or courtier showed low sprouts of sesame, onion, and garlic. Around the other side of the walled city, to the north, Sheba would later see fields of barley punctuated by stands of tall pomegranate, and she would hear a tale many times over about the head of the first man.

For now her party was considering the gates. There was nothing like them in Sheba, where palaces and even fortresses had many open doors of access. The queen took it for a sign that the king of Israel was concerned with protocol and legitimacy.

The structure of the gate was such that anyone entering must pass through a corridor of metal folded over against the stone city wall and partitioned into six chambers, each containing iron-armed guards in considerable number. Before entering, visitors surrendered their weapons into a small brick house. Out-of-favor prophets loitered just outside the gates, while just inside the walls of the city the king's justice was served.

The capital's walls were high and strong like the walls of the copper-mining town on the Gulf which the travelers had skirted in their long journey. This land was thick with fortified cities. King Solomon had stabled his thousands of horses behind the tightest defenses—in Gezer the high place, and Hazor, and Taanach, and Tell el-Hesi, and the chief defense town of them all, Armageddon.

The Sheban caravan approached: queen, women, youths, beasts, and men. Outside the court of Solomon in the City of David on the top of the last hill beyond the gate they stopped to gather themselves.

On the other side of the gate, crowds of workmen in white linen, merchants in costlier dress, and foreigners in every style of robe and turban thronged noisily about among the clatter of vehicles. Here were housewives, litigants, boys selling goat milk, farmers exchanging produce for tools, mule parties from Tirzah and Gaza arriving in fatigue and hunger and making anxious preparations to leave again. Ancient seers wailed out their terrible visions, wedged in, at the first steps of the city, among rough carts piled high with olive branches for the harvest festival. The young ignored them, full of the excitement of the coming feast. But still the stilted Hebrew incantations rose above the sounds of bells and wheels and pottery: "I abhor myself, I repent in dust and ashes!" "Ah, sinful nation, people laden with iniquity, seed of evildoers, corrupt from youth!" "Who is the wise man that he may understand this?"

On the curb two decrepit Jebusites were sitting and commiserating in an unprophetic vein. Life was hard in the old city since the Hebrews came, and they were grudgingly glad to be alive. Now they were reciting for the thousandth time the deed that had changed their lives, as always with scornful irony. How the old king or his commander, unable to take the impregnable walls of Jebus, had crawled like a reptile into the very center of the mighty city through the shaft of the well at Gehenna.

No, that's not what happened, the other interjected wearily, as usual. David and Joab only cut off the city's water supply.

The old argument rehearsed, they commenced to agree, with the detachment of military strategists, that victory in Jerusalem was the turning point. Without Zion, David would never have been able to make alliance with the Phoenicians. And without Tyre, Israel was no more than a band of poor but ambitious sheepmen.

"David never cared much for money," said one. Again they agreed, and repeated to each other that the shepherd never personally owned more than one talent of gold in his life.

"And that the gold crown of Milcom king of Amman bought with Uriah's death," rejoined the other. Nodding, scratching.

"But Solomon! Solomon, he's a different story." More nods.

"You know how much he's paying the workers at the arena?"

"The Temple mountain, they call it now."

"He's paying the Tyrians and the Egyptians together seventeen million dollars in gold! And I don't know how much for the rest of them."

"You don't say."

"What do you think of that?"

"What are you complaining about? You get the leavings in the beans, don't you?"

The one old man scratched his long-bearded face with a kind of devotion. "Life is hard in Jebus for a man whose children and grandchildren and great-grandchildren are strewn on the wind."

The other old man yawned, a gargantuan, body-wracking yawn.

Two young artisans were walking past the olive branch depot. A Jew of the Benjamin tribe and another of Manasseh, they treated one another like kin because they were descended, more than twenty generations before, from the same holy woman, Rachel. They were discussing the late war beyond the Great Sea, where the forces of Asia had succumbed to the forces of Achaea, and the Manassehite was recalling the death of one of the Achaean fighters.

63

"He fell in love with the Amazon queen, an opposing warrior."

"I wouldn't think an Amazon would be particularly attractive."

"Oh, no," said the first man, "an Amazon woman can be most striking." The other man looked at him hard for a moment, then signified acceptance on faith; they smiled together, and the first man continued.

"Well, Achilles was taken with this woman. He appreciated the warlike traits in her. But she was of the enemy, and he was committed to besting her. And best her he did, with an arrow to the heart. However—and this is what I wanted to tell you—as she fell, he took her in his arms for a last look, and at that moment the arrow struck that felled Achilles himself."

"Who killed Achilles?" asked the Benjaminite.

"Paris, I think," replied the other. "Though some Achaeans say it was the sun."

In good spirits the men of Rachel passed from the market of Israel and Judah into the smaller and more specialized market of the scribes.

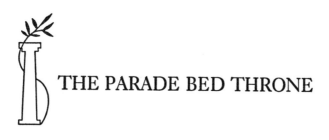

THE PARADE BED THRONE

WHEN SHE WAS CLOSE ENOUGH TO SEE the heat shimmering over the roofs of Jerusalem, Sheba left her light seashell litter for a litter of gold and retired behind her veils. Holding Son of Ia's hand but invisible to all others, her eyes misted with inspiration and power.

Her entrance into the city was signaled by a march of the fifty elephants single file, trunks raised, heavy and blasé. On their backs, tall left-handed mahouts with skin rosy as leather, their hair tied in golden cords, snapped long wands and uttered frightful cries. In the purpled splendor of the autumn morning the Shebans were agitated, the Judaeans delighted and curious. Black courtiers from beyond the Mountains of the Moon, who had rubbed their bodies in white and silver, preceded the soldiers of Sheba with their long, aristocratic faces, wearing the manes and ears of horses on their heads. Real chariot horses whinnied under the billowing standards.

At the center of the procession, servants carried the delegation's provisions: teff, broomcorn, millet, cress, castor, and safflower. Camels, lions, long-neck and river horse filed through the gates, followed by the less disciplined leopard and three great apes.

Last of all, by horseback and muleback, in palanquins and walking hand in hand, there followed six thousand maidens and youths, bright in silk clothes and turbans, dazzling in costume jewelry of agate, carnelian, chalcedony, and glass, and carrying with them the queen's most special gifts to the king in gold, emerald, sapphire, stone, and ebony.

To the city population crowding about, staring, pointing, and shouting, the beasts were a great diversion (and the children frolicked among them), but the most extraordinary thing was how closely and uncannily these many youngsters from Sheba resembled one another. More closely than brothers and sisters! And how they appeared to be exactly the same size, and the same age! And (strangest of all) how they seemed all to be of the same sex—but which, it could not be determined!

The queen in her robes of all white, showing not a single gem, mused behind her curtain nervously. She gave Solomon's man, Son of Ia, a teff cookie and sent him on his way, to convey her greetings to the king. He whispered as he left that he would slay a lion for her, if he had to. Not necessary, she smiled grimly. Her price was not death, but conquering wisdom.

Solomon was ready for her, calm, casual, firm. He had read her note of reply written in hot water and gall on skin, bound in wood. He could sense her world bead of lewd spice approaching. When she had been sighted on the southern road and a messenger dispatched to greet her, Solomon left court and went out to a simple and secret place in the brush of the fields behind Jerusalem for a period of undisturbed contemplation. His country throne was made of wood, with three steps leading up to the seat and a brief canopy to keep off the sun. It had a plain design of his seal, and a long sheaf of grain attached, for camouflage or luck. The king wore leather leggings and a rough wool cap, and in his hand he held the rod, globe, and star of his scepter, not much longer than the length of his forearm. He waited.

Presently the scribe Joseph ben Barakhya came riding out to him, leading the royal mare.

Son of Ia had connected with Son of Lightning. The scribe indicated that it was time for the king to repair to the public halls to meet his visitor. Solomon mounted, glancing with nostalgia at his rustic chair. Lions sometimes roamed the thistle country hereabouts.

On the way to the capital, Son of Lightning spoke of the

preparations that had been made upon the king's command. Great caskets of sticky Nubian millet beer awaited the queen of Sheba's party, and for the queen herself the most finely wrought posset cup of golden Syrian wine. The gifts were stacked on mules outside the palace ready for her people to take to their camp and enjoy. Silks and linens from Gaza, Assyria, and Lebanon. Sour purple. Tapestry from Ma-Wara-Nnar. Dresses stitched by the matchless Khorasani. From Iraq, sweet fruit, and from Mongolistan, winter melons. Green and blooming rose trees of Damascus, the city of light. And basins of the water of life from the spring at Siloe.

"She will be very dirty," Solomon said guardedly. Dust of the road required a ceremony of water hospitality. "She has been traveling for three years by ship and camel." But this traveler was different: a woman. Bathsheba's bath flashed through Solomon's mind. Trouble. And worse: in Solomon's language the word for camel bag and the word for chamber pot were one and the same.

Ben Barakhya reminded the king that this person's arrival was coinciding with the harvest festival. That she could therefore legitimately be isolated on ritual grounds, and purified in the huts by means of fire and water, as prescribed in the old writings.

"Ahum, yes, very good," said Solomon. He nodded his head.

Afar off, on the horizon, the silhouette of a big cat could be seen prowling at the riverbed. Solomon and his scribe rode at a gallop toward the place where he would soon find the travelling woman.

When they stopped at Adam's crossroads, Solomon turned again to ben Barakhya. "The Persians tell me," he said, "that this queen of Sheba sleeps on her throne, and I would like to know what that means. Do you know, Joseph? Your understanding is very great."

If wishes were beings, just then a creature of smokeless fire the desert people name an *afreet* might have been seen to whisper into Solomon's ear, "I will steal her throne for you."

But Barakhya spoke instantly on the subject, out of his old high Arabic knowledge, until a replica of this wonderful throne appeared to King Solomon in the fields behind Jerusalem more swiftly than a theft. "In Sheba the queen has a movable throne which is also a bed," the scribe related. "It moves in state; it is called 'parade bed.' Red gold of Sasu interwoven with green gold of Emu forms its foundation. Over its top she hangs a caged bird." The secretary stopped.

"Go on," said Solomon, putting a finger to his ear as if to scratch it.

"Yes. The size. It is of quite remarkable size. Perhaps eighty forearms in one direction."

"A bed like a great hall!" Solomon exclaimed, and thought, This woman is a very lioness. In his language this animal was chief over more than the beasts: there was a lion of intuition, and a lioness of language. A lion of the threaded needle, and a lioness that was the ovary. The pharaoh's daughter had taught him to know the lion in the sky, whose back formed a great starry curve; but now it seemed that Sheba's bed included even the bed of the powerful Egyptian within it. Solomon saw all the commonalty of lions and lionesses together in his mind, so flagrantly sensual, so solemn in their marriages, and he had a dim premonition of the commonalty that was Sheba.

"I feel the emanations of this bed even now," said Solomon.

"King," interposed ben Barakhya quickly, "construct such a one here in your own striped tents or in the huts of the Temple people or concealed among the harvest celebration booths or above the crystal floor of the bath. Place it in the House of the Forest of Lebanon or behind the golden curtain in the high house. The bed of the queen of the south has power indeed, but under your authorship its power will revert to you."

"Yes, perhaps you are right." The wind ruffled the stark faces of the thistles. Twilight darkened.

And the king of Israel built for himself a spacious throne-bed, inlaid with love. And he set it up inside his place of beauty, in the shade of a lightning-rod oak.

BOOK THE THIRD

KING AND QUEEN

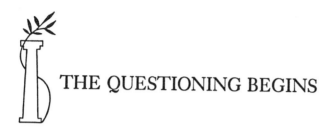

THE QUESTIONING BEGINS

DRUMS! TRUMPETS! HERE ARE THE KING and the queen at last! Solomon and Sheba are standing outside the unfinished Temple, his left hand in her right. Near them all around the broad Temple courtyard Israelites and Canaanites nudge Shebans for a better place to see and hear. Children sit irreverently on the steps of the Altar of Holocausts, from the top of which rises the smoke of heifers, ewes, rams, pigeon, and dove. Priests in blue linen stride importantly about. As far as one can see along the whole of Mount Zion's lucky threshing floor and over all the slopes beyond, citizens of Jerusalem are bustling and bumping into one another, clambering for seats on a wall, shouting and calling.

The queen is the most amazing woman any of these people have ever seen. Even with the elephants and camels parked safely out of sight her personal presence is stunning; she stands displaying herself like a star, arrogant as a river, glowing. Her eyes are clean of malice. A faint golden mist seems to radiate around her head, either from her smile or from the jewels draped in her hair and on her ears. A jeweled girdle around her soft hips holds a transparent veil folded for modesty, now rose, now blue. From her brow falls another veil, long and uneven, thin as a butterfly's wings. Over her bare heart rest eleven rings of jewels on eight chains. The ladies of Jerusalem are clutching their headscarves. Soon the smoke from the sacrifices will touch these unearthly eyes and make them blink. But Sheba is unafraid.

Solomon is uneasy. A heavy white wool cloak hangs over his leather kirtle and sandals. The skin on his face and arms is paler than hers, with a long wrinkle creasing his high forehead.

As energy flows erratically back and forth between them through their linked hands, he is looking at her and thinking of his high house. Soon it will be done. Soon the Ark of the Covenant, the Treaty Box, will be carried into its holy place, and the spirit of Ia will blaze out and take up residence. Soon these people, even here, these ruddy Israelites in the coarse linen they love so much, remembering Egypt and its finer linen, these people will be able to rejoice and feast around the Temple while the Aaronic caste of high priests communes inside with the sacred first writing of the tribes.

But for now the Temple is cold stone only, a pattern on a trestle board, a vision through the breast-high sight of a theodolite, the centered bubble of the level. The spirit of Ia, which the Jews call female, has not yet come.

Solomon signals to the heralds nearby that the questioning is about to begin. As befitting two grand and glorious monarchs, the visiting Queen Sheba will publicly interrogate the King Solomon. Her questions will be repeated loudly by a herald to the immense gathering; and then the monarchs will retreat for as long as necessary to consider the matter inside the stones and scaffolding of Ia's house; and then, when the enigma is solved, they will emerge together, and the heralds will cry out his answering speech.

The crowd falls silent.

Sheba clears her throat. Her first question concerns peace and war and global economics. The herald garbles it in the repetition.

"Oil," replies Solomon.

Sheba signals with her face that his answer is satisfactory, and the crowd lets out a roar of heady approval.

Around to the south of the incomplete Temple and behind some houses of the king's best men and courtiers, in a spacious apartment set aside for her until the Women's House of the Temple complex shall be completed, the princess of Egypt,

Solomon's first and only wife, is napping. Solomon was not displeased when she told him she chose to remain absent from this day's spectacle, on the pretext of a headache; later she will forget and tell him the reason was a stomachache. Now she is lying with her head on an outstretched arm, dreaming of the people in the sky, denying the reality of the visit of the queen of Sheba.

Sheba's second question is a request for the secret of life, death, and immortality.

The herald abbreviates it.

Solomon takes a step toward the Temple porch. He puts his large hand on the doorframe. A smile flits across his face.

"Flax," he says.

The queen of Sheba looks at him in dismay. Is he making fun of her? She turns like him to the unfinished masonry to think. Through the high outer door she catches sight of two golden cherubs resting against the inner doors: strange birdlike felines possessed of a touch of humanity, something higher—the sphinxes of Egypt. Then she understands. Solomon has learned from his wife. He is speaking of the somatic immortality of the Egyptian dead, whose hollowed bodies are laden with spices and painstakingly wrapped, in . . . flax.

The answer does not please her, but it is not serious enough a breach to register an official complaint. She shows conflict. Half the crowd cheers.

At the very farthest point from which the king and the queen can still be seen, there is a man standing and listening with a slight frown. Perhaps it is his customary expression, or perhaps he is looking right into the souls of those two small, distant figures, their voices amplified by servants. His broad chest naked, his left arm akimbo and resting beneath his heart, his right forearm supporting him against a small fence pole, it is Son of Ia, Solomon's messenger to Sheba in caravan, and herald of her arrival.

The queen of Sheba declares her third question. "What is the power of sex?"

For this Solomon needs no intermission. At once he steps close and touches a finger to her eyelash. Black powder comes off. He looks at his fingertip. "Kohl."

73

At this the woman is decidedly irritated. She knows the separation between her sexual nature and the ceremonious eye makeup. But the crowd sees it like Solomon, and she is down for the decision.

By previous agreement, the first set of questions is over. King and queen walk around the northern perimeter of the Temple to the small residences of the Temple people, where they are ushered into a priestly hut.

Outside the hubbub is great. Questions are analyzed and rehashed and recorded, with some holding that the ones are better than the others, and others arguing that the match between magician and magicienne is still even. Solomon's scribes praise his pithy style, the punning word, deflation, and concreteness. Sheba's style is vaunted as nobler, loftier, more relevant. There are many good-hearted arguments.

Inside the hut Solomon and Sheba look at each other with measuring glance. They nibble on pigeon. A servant places dishes of cut apples in front of them, and withdraws.

"So how are you, King?" Sheba says.

"I'm good," answers Solomon. "Understanding. Bringing my wisdom to bear. The important thing is justice. How justice is in my kingdom, that's how I am."

He's a little pompous, she thinks, but at least he's not always going to be so terse. "Funny," she says, "I understand what you mean. But I would say love. How love is among my people, that's how I am, that's who I am." By the suggestion in her own words her eyes instinctively go to the king's loins. The cloak has fallen back and his knees show out from under the purple leather. They tremble. "But you don't understand what I mean by love. And I don't understand what you mean by justice."

"Ha!" exclaims the king. "Nicely said!" He pops a crescent of apple into his mouth and savors its sweetness. "But perhaps we should continue here, without the heralds and the people's cheers to come between us. You seem to be more relaxed." In fact it is he who is more relaxed, but this does not seem to him a crucial distinction.

But the queen of Sheba is suspicious. Is Solomon trying to take advantage of her? He is a little larger than she, a little

74

heavier (though she is tall and strong), and this puts the fear of force in her heart. What would her advisers have her do? Can she handle him without the mass of popular opinion as a guide, a mediation, a control? As she delicately pulls the flesh from the wing of a pigeon she decides she will put aside the "hard questions" for a time, and try him on some enigmas every child in Sheba knows.

"All right, Mr. Wisdom," she says, looking sexy and feeling crafty, "what is the longest straight line?" Her pigeon bones discarded, a pretty hand masks her half-closed eyes.

Solomon stiffens, and he shifts in his chair. But the question is easy.

"This globe of earth under our feet spins around a straight line piercing its center," he replies. "And that is the longest straight line we know of, by God!"

"God?" she repeats. "Interesting. I shall ask you about 'God' in public. But first, that which is prior to 'God.'" And quickly she continues, "What begins in five, goes to nine, becomes one, and ends at two?"

Solomon doesn't seem to know. Her casual remark about God has set off a bit of a smoke haze in his brain. He searches her face, her eyes, her lips, for the answer. Then he gives in to his own confusion, and lets his sight haze over altogether. Still looking at her he sees only the rhythm of her body's movements, her spine, as it were, through the back of her dissolved flesh. But soon her flesh gradually reimposes itself on the king's consciousness, and with it the answer to the riddle.

"For five days the woman is separated, until she conceives; then for nine months she carries; then the one inside her is born, and cries for two breasts."

"Solomon!" cries out the queen of Sheba, in petulant delight. "How did you guess that?" The king chuckles.

"I have another," she continues. "There is an enclosure. When one gate is open, nine are closed. When nine are open, one is closed. What is it?"

But this is not difficult for Solomon. He can read in the bristling of the hair along her arm and the raised skin under her jewels that the subject matter is not different but the same. In this short time Solomon has conceded to Sheba sovereignty over the world of women, and by this mental act he has gained a certain strength over her.

"The babe in the womb has only one opening to the world," says Solomon, "that is through its belly. But the adult woman has ten gates to and from the world. And, my dear Queen, those I see of yours are very pleasant."

For the first time in her life Sheba feels an antagonism between her queenship and her femaleness; the one is ruffled, the other mollified. Solomon has this same separation in himself, she thinks. The way he tries to speak of the intimate is wrong, is threatening. It is as if (as she had guessed immediately, from just seeing him) he is not interested in love for its own sake, but for the sake of other ends: power, revenge, gold; what exactly, she doesn't know.

A tiny autumn wind blows. Sheba arranges to become cold. A servant in the priestly hut brings her a large goatskin cloak, and she hugs it tightly about her chest. That feels better. She looks at Solomon blankly. Counts the hangings on the walls. And asks him why there are seven days in the Judaean week.

Solomon's shaggy eyebrows rise. "The moon is the answer," he begins, and Sheba shivers.

"Seven times the light of the moon equals once the light of the sun." Sheba sits forward. "And in seven days the moon lives through one of its lifetimes. The Hebrews watch the moon very closely."

"Is this true?" asks Sheba breathlessly.

"By my bones and ivory!" swears Solomon. And then he tells her about the ceremony of the new moon: about the witnesses who come each month from all parts of the country to a certain courtyard in Jerusalem to be feasted and questioned by the elders; and about the torch that is lit on the Mount of Olives when the elders are satisfied that the new moon has really been seen; and how the torches are lit, from that light, on the summits of all the mountains throughout the land, announcing the new month to all Israel.

"How interesting," says Sheba. "But of course, your women don't—and what a fascinating expedient.

"And the week comes from the moon . . . fascinating. Now that you have lost the main connection, you establish others, which are, in their way, I am sure, almost as satisfying. But tell me, do you still see the moon for what it's worth?"

"Tell me what the moon is worth, Sheba," says Solomon, with something like sincerity coloring his irony.

So Sheba speaks of the moons: the four moons that have hung in the sky, and fallen in their turn, and been replaced. The moon as the final resting place of all dead matter from the earth. The moon as mother of tides and lust, of the dropping of children, and of all that bubbles or shines white, in life and death. Solomon takes in a breath sharply. He feels a coldness, a threatening, a confirmation of the subtle dread he began to have at the moment when the arrival of the queen became an imminent reality. She knows too much for a woman, and her knowledge is dangerous.

"Do you then worship the moon?" he says guardedly.

"Oh, no," says Sheba.

"The sun?" he says.

Now the woman-queen recomposes herself, and sits back on the rough cushion some priestess or priest has allowed to be there for her, and she begins to discuss the beliefs of Sheba. She does not intend to speak with entire candor about this, however, until after the man-king has begun speaking with openness of his own God or gods.

But as Sheba speaks of her mother and of the priestess-guardians of the writings and of the revels, Solomon's thoughts are precisely there, with his own so different divinity. As she speaks of the midsummer night, he sees in his mind's eye the Old Man. As she speaks of the palm tree and of the silver and gold glinting of moon and sun on the forest brook, he thinks of the fire the old teacher saw in an acacia bush. And as she pronounces the names of Ethiopia of the high and wild cliffs and of Yemen of the fertile fields and of Zimbabwe the golden, the many names by which his God are known are rushing through Solomon's head in a torrent. Ia, he is thinking, and YH, Yud Heh, YHVH, Iabe, Iahw, JHWH, Jebuotao, Jehuovao. Finally the pressure overwhelms him. She is all loveliness. Her speech is like the messages of unspeakable birds.

"Iaooué!" he says, at last.

"What?" says Sheba.

And the exalted dove flies into the flapping opening of the hut. And the boy and girl grown up to possess the keys of all the kingdoms lean forward and take a fragile little kiss of each other.

"Now we must stop," Solomon then declares, with a preemptive assumption of dominion over time.

So Solomon and Sheba, with all their vast entourages, retire to separate encampments. Night falls on Jerusalem. A tall cypress points to the sky beside the Temple and everything else sleeps.

But soon enough morning arises again over Arabia and Persia, dripping slowly up through eggshells and other sky litter of the dream angels, pink, red, and yellow, hailing the flamegold of the only great car. Sheba leaves her tent while it is still blue-black night and watches the sun from a hilltop.

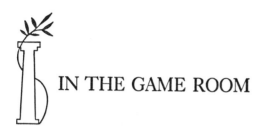

IN THE GAME ROOM

THE CROWD IN THEIR MANY BEDS AWAKE with the clattering of slippers and breaking fast. All Jerusalem is thrilled by the presence of Sheba with Solomon, the dimonarchate, excited by love and power. Some hope they will marry. Some fear her. Just to be alive on this day is an act of grace.

The first cloud of autumn drifts through a cool sky and below it the people sift back toward the threshing floor. Here an elder wearing Indian linen his bewigged wife has freshly washed and pressed. Here a Damascene outlaw from Rezon's group, dandy in white wool, toting a skin of red wine. Worn sandals of the road. Women with black eyes. The gleam and clink of copper and wood. The Israelites gradually take their places.

For her second appearance, the queen of Sheba wears saffron orange, the color of gnosis. King Solomon is wrapped in a black nomad robe, with a soft Egyptian crown on his head, paying no attention to his bicep where a bee has stung him during the night. A Babylonian woman runs in front of the royal platform at the porch, gaudy and happy in a many-colored dress, a pied tapestry like the day itself.

The scribes wait with brushes poised.

"Who gave God a name?" asks Sheba before the ten thousands.

Behind her, in the shadow of a tent polestring, Sheba's first minister is watching. From where she stands, she sees the left side of the queen's face and her left shoulder. She sees the queen's long veil fastened at the crown like an Arab's; she sees the queen's features delicate and exquisite, like the statues of Benin. She sees Sheba's braided hair and her straight nose, almost squared at the bone, not rounded. She sees the queen of Sheba bow to Solomon, and she feels her pleasure.

Solomon takes Sheba's arm and they step together inside the Temple portico to divert themselves while he thinks. Her voice is like the voice of a spirit, but he needs a man or a djinn—or even a demon!—to tell him the answer. Ha! That's it! He motions the heralds at the door to take his answer out.

"It was the devil who first named God's name."

The people in the great arena cheer and exult. They pass his words from lip to lip: "It was the Devil who first named the name of God. . . ." "It was The Devil. . . ."

Sheba too appreciates this answer for its rhythm, its euphony, its cantillation, though she has no idea whatsoever what "devil" means. Hers was a land without demons or witches. Generation upon generation there had been a stasis of individual and society from the sea of Atlantis to the Sofalan coast. It was only the final expansion of horizons, the same which had brought her to Jerusalem, that had engendered corruption. Subtle havoc leaked into Eden with the bags and packs of safety pins and forks. As Sheba's magical herbs and resins spread ineluctably north by trade route through the deserts of Arabia and the outer Nile, straining toward the metropolitan northern centers, the howling spirits of those intermediary places flooded in through the clay doors ajar of the happy villages. It was said by Nilotics and Arabs that none but the devil and his grotesque minions inhabited the wild empty spaces between the lands of Solomon and the lands of Sheba—the bad, wasted land where one time the moon they called "Sahara" dropped out of the sky onto the earth and left only death.

Then the storm gods of the north came pushing in, to challenge the queen goddess of heaven. Sheba was both innocent and sophisticated. She was inspired by them. She felt justification for her own restlessness in the western Zeus, in IHVH speaking from a volcano, in Indra of the east. To her mind all gods were good, for the world was good, and she saw them as so many lovers. She hungered for the change, the movement, the progress, the revolution that they suggested. But her hope that they would be good lovers to her and her people was tempered with fear. She understood from her princes and advisers that she should reserve judgment.

Out of the confusion in her brain between the voices of naiveté and of cynicism, Sheba fetched out the premise that she was, as an individual, unique. That Solomon was unique. That the interaction between them would be unique. At this moment she is looking at Solomon with a soft eye and inclined to trust him. The way he says "devil" makes her laugh. His devil seems like a small thing, cute, like a pet animal. The evil that his devil implies is not real to her.

"What is evil?" she says.

"The eyes of the Lord in every place monitor good and evil, and in them is the definition."

"Are eyes or ears superior?" she says.

"The hearing ear, and the seeing eye, the Lord hath made both," he says. "Degrees of deafness and blindness, these are man's province, and measurable."

"What is the most powerful organ of the body, Solomon?"

"Death and life are in the power of the tongue!"

At last I am hearing Solomon's true voice, she thinks, and is glad. And she asks him, "How are body and spirit connected?"

Solomon says, "The baseness of spirits is derived from their bodies. The nobility of bodies is derived from their spirits."

Sheba pulls the saffron veil of her robe over her head in a gesture of nervous excitement and announces she has no more questions for the day.

So king, queen, and their retainers retire to the hall of justice in Solomon's palace. There a tesselate game board has been set up for them between a double throne, and Solomon and Sheba sit down to while away the rest of the afternoon in privacy. But the spirit of opposition is not relaxed. He swears by his white markers, saying his tribe the Hebrew was named after ivory. She swears by her black tokens, saying that alone of all woods in the world, ebony is uncorruptible by termites. Keen to learn a new game, Sheba at first wins, but then later loses. In anger she sweeps all the intricate lace patterns of stone and wood off the board with a long-fingered hand.

Solomon laughs at her. Sheba narrows her eyes. And begins questioning him in earnest.

"How do you dare challenge the absolute continuity of mother and daughter?" she demands.

Solomon's eyes still laugh. Calling for a servant, he requests boiled eggs.

This makes Sheba furious. Standing, brushing a stray ivory stone from her lap, stalking the hall of judgment become a game room, she turns to the king on his throne and demands to know how an economic system based on paternity can possibly be reliable.

Growing sober, and more sober, and finally terrible in his solemnity, Solomon replies in a loud voice that there is scientific accuracy in fatherhood.

"The blood of the child adheres to the bone of the father, living or dead," he declares majestically.

"O Illâhat!" moans Sheba, and sinks into a faint.

The servants gasp, and run toward her, but Solomon pushes them away, and bends over the woman, and lifts her with care. Together they pace the shiny black and white floor until color returns to her cheek. In her ear he whispers encouragement, not to be afraid of the way of the fathers, for "fear is a betrayal of the comforts reason offers."

When she is herself again, not embarrassed, still angry, Solomon announces he has a hard question for her.

"We are erecting a pillar in the Temple," he says, "which will be cut from one great tree. Now when this pillar is standing, of girth such and such, with scrollwork and capital such and such, how will you know which end was the original root, and which end was the branches?"

Sheba is on her throne again, opposite Solomon. With one hand she is making patterns of the ivory and ebony on the game board.

"I will throw your pillar into the sea," she says. "And the end that was the root will sink."

And she gives him a defiant smile.

*　　*　　*

And thus the days pass and then the weeks. Winter drops from the sky with the narrowing sun and closes the fragrant white oleander and whispers of cold. In the afternoons after the public morning ceremony Solomon and Sheba lie in double palanquins talking, talking to one another. A sword hangs between them. They come no closer than a rainbow through a prism on a whitewashed wall comes to the great arc of colors that heralds the end of a flood.

One night, just to amuse himself, Solomon decides to try out on his wife the kind of question Sheba has been asking him.

He summons her from her apartments; he calls her a pet name. And then he asks, with sudden severity, "What is the meaning of life?"

The Egyptian thinks a moment. She brings a hand to her lip and tilts her head to a side, her hips moving the opposite way, not unattractively. Then she settles back, and bats her lashes at him.

"Life is addiction, Solomon," she says.

"Get out of here!" he roars.

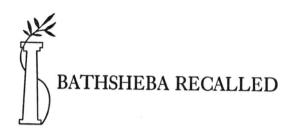

BATHSHEBA RECALLED

On another bright silver-light day in young Jerusalem Sheba stands up before the multitudes and, adjusting her girdle, asks Solomon, "What is the wisdom of your God, and what is your God's understanding, and what is this God's knowledge?" And Solomon answers her, and in appreciation of his wit and profundity she makes a fist of her hand and her long nails glint in the sun. The scribes record. And she goes on: "What is the beginning of wisdom? . . . How is wisdom related to understanding? . . . How is instruction related to wisdom and to understanding? . . ." And Solomon answers, and his answers are applauded by the people, and recorded. And she continues: "Solomon, what do you say we receive from our fathers and what from our mothers? . . . And what is it we return to our mothers, and what to our fathers? . . . And how shall we be rewarded and punished, by your system of accounting, after the inheritance of our mothers and our fathers?" And Solomon hesitates, and then he speaks, and answers her, and the scribes record his words and bind them into a long book, a book of books.

And the queen has many more questions to ask the king concerning wisdom and understanding and the powers of the mind, and of trials and testimony in the exercise of judgment, and of negations of thought and negations of action and what value is to be placed upon the secret works of men. And of this, the greater part is recorded in a scroll they call the *Proverbs* of Solomon. And what is not there was in one of the lost books.

The aging Bathsheba sits in her comfortable palm-filled apartment on Mount Moriah. Married to King David when she was an unripe fig, she is still attractive and sociable. This afternoon a servant girl is combing her thick hair into a braided "bird's nest" of loops, while the queen mother herself looks over some writing on a roll of parchment.

In recent years it has become her habit to follow the teachings of the prophet of Shiloh. The prophet's accusations against her son King Solomon are rather harsher than she would make, but she finds it quietly comforting to read them.

Slowly Bathsheba becomes aware that the serving girl is humming under her breath a popular song from the city. With a pang she remarks the main characters in the song: her son, her daughter-in-law, a lioness. And she begins to brood. The Egyptian is such a thorn. That marriage is such a bad one. A fast woman! She feeds Solomon lotus and cottonseed oil to make him sterile! But what better to expect when the most eligible man in the world marries an heiress out of his archenemies!

And for all that, thinks Bathsheba, he rebels against me. I, who went to my husband on his deathbed, when he was rattling with the cold (though his mind still lucid), and reminded him of his intention to make our son king. She puts down the prophet's scrap of parchment sadly.

All for that old business; there's not another soul that holds the thing against me. Israel was on our side, for I was young and virtuous. And who could hold it against the lovely David? Bathsheba has forgotten the terror she felt when the prophet Nathan was threatening to have her stoned.

But she remembers clearly the night the girl-steward impugned her dying husband's virility, and he called for Bathsheba his favorite wife, and used her then so harshly, so like a young man, that she had to go to the bathhouse and dry herself before the sunrise thirteen times.

What a man he was, David! And what a problem is Solomon.

* * *

Solomon takes Sheba for a walk outside the city walls. They walk in a southeasterly direction until they come to a spot of lush fertility, the King's Garden, washed by three fresh streams. As he gathers up armfuls of vegetables and herbs for her to take back to the cooks in the Sheban camp, she studies the movements of his lean muscled thigh.

"You hate your mother," says Sheba bluntly.

"How do you know that?"

"You flinched when I used the word 'mother' in the questioning. Though you answered beautifully enough."

"Would you like some leeks and garlic?"

"Her name sound likes mine. I wonder about her."

Now it has been said that the queen of the south had had many lovers. From the earliest time she had known how to love, and she had loved well, and richly, and with a full pleasure that made her body of one piece with the wind and the air in the balmy days. She appreciated the gift. But she was not altogether satisfied with it.

She imagined a lover through whom the past of her centuries would be annihilated, a lover larger than love. It was like a thirst for death, but it was not that. At the edge of the abyss, from the jaws of the beast, she anticipated stepping back and snatching the prize that would give her life unto the myriad generations its meaning and worth.

On his part, Solomon had warmed to his powerful female rival because there was something in her that he needed for his own most private, gardenside reasons.

The behaviors of his adulterous parents David and Bathsheba; of the brother Absalom who had dared desecrate the harem—the man David's only legal possession!—and the executed brother Adonijah who had merely suggested it . . . Such all were an unresolved tangle in the heart of the precocious prince. Nowhere in the Hebrew legends and mythologies was there instruction for him in the matter of sex.

Sheba, to Solomon, had knowledge and surety in her veins. She could take up the boy-man with an authority his mother did not have, nor the Egyptian bride, nor any other woman in this league of warriors and their conquered wives.

And so she does just that, now, in the garden, reassuring and pampering, and cajoling him; and she takes him into her plum-brown arms; and he bows his head there, and lets out a heavy sigh. He will never actually tell her the whole story of David and Bathsheba—or that of Absalom, or of Adonijah and Joab—for the bass-note understanding in him about all this has changed in her presence, and there is no need to. But he begins this day, and he continues for a long time, to blurt out fragments of the story, as bits of the dilemma arise to his reason.

"David was the seventh son. Everyone loved him. I am the youngest of many more children than that. I was never close to him. I worshiped him, like the rest."

"I have heard many stories about your father David since I have been here," says Sheba, "from Brother of Ia and Judge's Pause."

"Did you know he was picked by the prophet to be king when he was just six years old, and with no one in his family putting him forward?"

"So I have heard."

Solomon turns away frowning, as if hiding something. "But I was made king by my mother. If not for her, the kingdom would have gone to Adonijah, for he was then the oldest. Soon after, I killed him."

"One takes one's throne as one can."

Solomon looks intently at the queen of the south. Can she possibly understand? "It isn't that so much. It's Bathsheba herself. She is illegitimate."

Sheba's face wrinkles sympathetically. "What on earth do you mean?"

"I mean," says Solomon, suddenly doubting himself, "that Bathsheba was just a commoner. She took that name—Daughter of the Seven, Daughter of the Oath—when she decided to leave Uriah and achieve my father. She pretended to his legitimacy. *He* was the seventh. And all there was to swear over was lust! My mother was a whore!"

"Oh, is that it?" Sheba says, smiling. Slowly and carefully she sits herself down on the ground, placing her back against a round rock. She takes a bite of cake of injara she has brought with her. (Up the hill in the capital the king's latest witticism is going around: "Unarmed wisdom can deliver a city from siege.")

Solomon looks nakedly sincere. His nose is long, and the features on his face bony and handsome. Though he stoops a bit, and is perhaps nearsighted (from the way he peers), Sheba thinks he is fine and interesting to look at; she finds him soulful, and keeps watch on the frequent changes of his face few others notice.

"Solomon, my dear," she continues after a while, "you do not realize, so I must tell you: love is good." The woman has wealth in her eyes. "Full-bodied lust is the best of all. Without it, there is no meaning of good."

But this is too much for the king. "Bathsheba and my father were adulterers!" he stammers, his voice choked.

"Don't be stupid, Solomon," says Sheba, chewing. "David had dozens of mistresses and wives. Your mother had two husbands. Why should hers bother you more than his?"

Solomon stops; his face is screwed up and angry. Then he relaxes slightly. He sits down too, not far from her, touching the grass with a soft hand.

"Anyway we don't have adultery in Sheba. Or whores, for that matter."

"My mother said she was going to kill me, when I was three years old."

"Good. That makes more sense than adultery."

"All I did was say that there was no such thing as an honest, righteous girl."

"Your old teacher who gave you adultery didn't mean for you to take it so hard."

"What do you know about Moses?"

"His first wife was a Sheban, named Tharbis."

"Oh!"

Sheba goes on. "A princess. She delivered the Burnt Face country into the hands of Egypt under General Moses. Because she loved him. That was before he got into Jewish liberation. He married again, of course. That's why I know about him. And about Egypt, too, though their ways are nothing like ours.

They've always looked to us as a sister civilization, because in spring our melting snows flood their river, and they can eat. Here, would you like some cake?"

Solomon almost actually smiles. "All I want right now is relief from the pain I feel when I think about them. You know, before I met you, I always thought more about my mother Bathsheba than about any other woman."

"I can imagine."

"Even than my wife," Solomon admits.

Sheba checks a thought about Solomon's wife, about whom she has mostly secondhand information, and says only, "I understand."

"I believe you do. When I look at you I can almost understand, too, why my mother and my father came together in lawless passion."

The woman smiles in her eyes at him and moves a slim knee.

"Your father must have understood it. You were born of his understanding."

"Yes, yes, of course, but I have never come even close to his kind of love. He was a genius in love, as in everything. But still they condemned him. All my teachers took Nathan's view of it."

"Why?"

"Why? I never thought to ask why. It must be because the Israelites are so tough. They broke company with life in Egypt by main force, and have been fighting everyone on all sides ever since."

"You are great, Solomon, and your people are great," says Sheba. "They bring swords on their thighs to bed with them at night. David was a warrior, but he caught the star Bathsheba threw."

"When I look at you, Sheba, I see the wisdom of love. I see in your arm, in your forehead, in your knee, a way of life that is in no way known to us here."

"You see the rule of women. Women of beauty. The rule of love."

"It is so hard—! The difference between us is so great! Yet to be with you is such refreshment!"

Together they rise and cross back through the valley.

90

Walking in the fresh grass, speaking together, their heads close, both feel the cells of their brains fountaining in joy.

With Solomon in conversation I will pass my days, thinks Sheba, speaking on a long immortal afternoon that fades toward the asymptote of time.

THE DIFFERENCE BETWEEN MALE AND FEMALE

SOLOMON AND SHEBA RUN A FOOTRACE. Sheba wins by a hair. Solomon grumpily suggests she had some kind of advantage. Sheba laughs.

Sipping cool pomegranate juice, they settle back into the palanquins. On and on they speak, with no way to tell, when they are alone, whether what they say to each other is the highest wisdom or *folie à deux*.

"Solomon, what is the difference between male and female?"

"What!?" laughs the king, with abundance written on his brow and an arcane curl of his lip.

"Why do you laugh," says Sheba, "at my hardest question?" And the queen sits back and starts to describe her native land. She tells him about the people there: the ancient venerated librarian, the nameless priestesses of the different ways, the callous-armed pythoness and her circle, the dancers in color, the mothers. How it is women who choose their men, and own the game and the gold and the cattle and the groves, and allot all to their daughters. How, long before, the wise women discovered the way to make raggee grow in the ground, and how they still oversee this activity.

"In Israel I see that your women are small and your men large, and I understand you do not allow your women to love or to work as we do in Sheba, and you say they are not fit for it.

93

"We have a different male and female in Sheba, that is clear."

And leaning forward, and pointing one finger of her left hand diagonally to the sky, she asks, "But what is the truth? What is really female, and what is really male? How would you distinguish them?"

Then the queen causes to be brought before herself and Solomon the six thousand Sheban youths, maidens and boys, all precisely the same age, entirely alike in stature, and wearing clothing of their own or of the other sex indiscriminately. The crowd of them are a lovely sight: rippling and iridescent as sand and shells.

"Take them clothed, as they are, and tell me who is the female among these," says Sheba sweetly, and sits back again.

"Very simple," says Solomon. He rings a bell at his side to summon Gift of the King, the eunuch. By Solomon's direction, the eunuch fetches a large quantity of nuts and sweets which he casts at the children, one by one; and with his practiced eye he throws the morsels of food in such a way as to shock the modesty of the little girls (who reach for their clothes) and provoke the bravado of the little boys (who make adjustments in the holding of their legs); and then the eunuch pours water from a basin onto the Shebans' hands—onto the left hands of the girls (who moisten their right before putting the water to their faces) and onto the right hands of the boys (who take such water up directly).

The eunuch is dismissed, and Solomon with assurance separates the little Sheban host into two camps. Sheba protests.

"But you depend on the eye of a sexless one!"

"Did you forbid it?"

Sheba gathers two of the little Shebans into her arms and kisses them, and smells their heads. The worst is as she feared: these men have undermined these women. Given the natural ways of love unpleasant names. Tied each woman closely to one man so that the father of their children will always be known. Put all the property, from the earth to the stars, in the hands of the fathers and their oldest sons. And Solomon, for all his wisdom in the ways of the Old Man, will not or cannot be honest about it. This she had realized in her body when his absurd remark about the blood and bones of paternity (which he seemed to believe!) made her faint. And now she has finally realized it in her brain, when the spectacle of her six thousand human jewels failed to evoke from Solomon simple admiration. Indeed, the naked eye, the eye of love, could not distinguish between the female and the unfemale of them, so erotic were they all. But the king called in the sexless one to help him, that technician of the male-dominated society.

Does Sheba hate Solomon? Strangely enough, she finds him irresistible. That he should value her, and at the same time think little of all women, sets up a highly charged alternating circuit in the system. She will reform him. She will save him. She will redeem all womanhood for him. And then, with his power and wealth and wisdom, she and he will reverse the disestablishment of her sex.

"Sheba, I think there is still something great and enormous I don't know about your country, and I want to know it."

Sheba is on her guard.

"What do you lack here, Solomon? Food? Clothes? Tools? Workers? Everything you have is excellent. I delight in your speech even as you descend and arise in your disposition. What concerns you of your sister Sheba's home?"

"I think you have something in mind," he replies dryly.

"Something in mind. . . . What do you want to talk about? The handedness?"

Solomon slaps his thigh with satisfaction. "The handedness—yes! The mahouts!"

Sheba is impressed despite herself. "That's right, the mahouts. They held the elephant whips in their left hands, and you noticed."

"What is the meaning of this phenomenon, my dear?"

The queen stretches out her magnificently angled left arm and looks at it. "The meaning is self-evident. In Sheba, in Ophir, from high mountains to long river, throughout the gold country—we are as left-handed as you in Israel and Hit and Aram are right-handed."

"Is this of deep and lasting significance?"

"Perhaps. I think so. Yes."

And they speak of the left and the right. Solomon is as acquainted as Sheba with the moon that rises each day in its circle a little to the left, and he knows like her that life prospers more fully under the waxing moon, at the righter side. And so they agree that the right hand is thus everywhere stronger than the left. But Sheba has a point to add.

"This left is called, in Sheba, the side of justice. And we believe that what it lacks of the strength of the right is compensated for by its proximity to the seat of understanding in the heart. And so we call it the better side. Thus in the education of small children, and the disposition of hunters and craftsmen. We are a left-handed civilization."

Solomon regards the woman before him. Her personal left-handedness is invisible. Yet he understands—why or whence he cannot say—that this matter of left and right is of great importance. The different choice their two peoples have made might make them, he stops to think, almost too different even to communicate. He feels vertigo. And then, impetuously, to stave off the dizziness, really, Solomon takes Sheba's left hand and says, "Will you steal my heart from out its left side and put it in a mirror, and make me mad?"

Sheba caresses his hand. "Oh, Solomon," she says, "you are joking. I know there is no madness under the sun but what your father David put on to escape a hard squeeze in Gath. It is my favorite of all the David stories. The time he was caught with the sword of the giant in the giant's own land, and faced death until a little ranting and frothing won him safe passage out again. You told me it yourself."

"Sweet Sheba," continues Solomon, "in the end I will go mad to escape my own sword. Speak to me of love."

Are Solomon and Sheba in love? Is this love talk? Or is it just the pursuit of wisdom that has led them to each other? Sheba can tell him, if she wishes, that love is the oldest stratagem for the obtaining of truths and knowledge. Close to the seat of intelligence there are no other tools but those of love, and no other ores.

Benaiah, Son of Ia, has a way of always catching the sun on his face. He has taken a liking to the mysterious first minister from Sheba. But, by chance, he approaches her at an inauspicious moment. Some kind of tiny demon has attacked and undermined her female sections, and she is in a constant itch. Naturally she can't speak of it. Certainly not to these big males.

The flirtation is frustrating.

"Don't you know a kindred soul?" asks Benaiah plaintively.

"Maybe I've kindred enough," replies the dark woman, and waits for him to leave so she can leave separately.

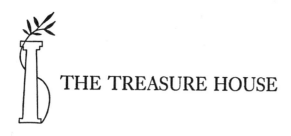

THE TREASURE HOUSE

"By the way, Sheba," says Solomon, "how do you come to have six thousand subjects born in the same hour? How many souls are in your empire?"

"Twelve hundred million," she says.

"No, I can't believe that," says the king.

"Would you prefer to believe that the women of Sheba conceive in unison, once a year and once only?"

The dark pupils of the king's eyes expand. He strokes his beard.

"It is the truth. And I have none greater," the queen remarks casually. "Now I suppose I must ask you something equally sublime."

"Go ahead."

Sheba takes a deep breath and puts her hand on the hangings of the hut. She pauses. Then: "What is the All-in-All, what does It consist of?" says the pilgrim to wisdom.

Solomon King is not stumped by this for an eye blink, not for a standing up and a sitting down. He replies immediately and in a hypnotic voice, "Space-time. Life. Speech. . . ."

"Is that it?"

"There is one thing more I don't want to say right now. But I promise I will let you hold it in your hand in a little while."

Solomon paces around his chamber alone. It is night. The moon casts a shadow of cypress on the sleeping mat. He goes to the treasure house. There he rests his eyes on the spectacle of works of art from every corner of the trading world: gold, silver, bronze, copper, jewelwork of finesse and charm: it is all there. He overbroods.

What shall he give Sheba?

Many understand the greed of Solomon, whose empire is the richest or second richest on earth. But few know that the secret of this collection is the telling of fortunes. In each object inheres the excellence of its creators who exist in some particular place and culture. And it is intuitions of these real men, in real societies, that Solomon seeks now, as he wanders with apparent aimlessness over a marble and gold checkerboard floor beneath three storeys of divinatory objects.

The array is comprehensible only to the wise king. It spreads up and outward, for the building is wider at the roof than on the ground. Outside, three rows of pomegranate and lily pillars support the overhanging upper portions. Great gold sphinxes guard the doors at the narrow end of the building, where the greatest treasure in the house is hid from all but initiates. Solomon climbs a narrow staircase to the uppermost tier, where he plucks a small object from its spot.

The next day he shows it to her. She grasps it eagerly, and examines it with a keen eye. Mineral, vegetable, and animal substances have been worked together into a masterpiece of integrated parts that suggests a great, benevolent, and universal hierarchy. Twelve different kinds of small pieces reflect darkly (Edomite copper? Sumerian clay? shell from the Great Sea? polished hardwood of Ebla?) in a pattern that interweaves and beguiles and merges with progressively larger and lighter pieces, flowing in discernible lines and chains. The queen of Sheba sees white aromatic woods carved into roses, and Sudanese ivory in concentric spheres, and distant Indian coral, and the flame knobs of old bones faded with the years by blood to an embarrassed pink. "It is an emblem of paternity," says Solomon. "It represents the souls of three hundred and seventy-five patriarchs, from as many different tribes."

The queen of Sheba rolls the vibrant thing around in her hands. How much conjuring can be done on such a mind-revealing bauble, of such workmanship, of such materials! She places the necklace around her neck.

"What can I give you for your Temple?" says the queen.

"What do you think we need?"

The queen considers. She is feeling pleased with this Solomon, and with the house he is building, that has as much prowess in its foundations as in its citadel.

"Red and green stair steps," she says. "Red for the gold of Sasu and green for the gold of Emu. Yes, and balustrades, too. The heads of lion and lioness in striped brown and white stone. Book bindings."

"You are very good," the king replies.

And she leans toward him, as if for a kiss, and whispers, "What is the name of thy most high God, O Solomon?"

Solomon waits a long time before answering. Will he lose his power to her if he speaks, as Re lost his to Isis? Considering this, he makes a very slight modification of the words forming back of his throat. And then he says aloud, "The most high, in thy language, dear Sheba, is the To Be without Non-being. . . . Dost understand?"

Understand? She half closes her eyes and lets her lips tremulously open, bathed in admiration. As wisdom and science are one thing to King Solomon, so truth and love are indistinguishable for the queen of Sheba. Beneath the magical necklace, the curve of her breast stops his heart.

And he touches her, and kisses her. And slowly, with a gesture of infinitesimal awkwardness, shrugs away his cloak.

She smells the moisture of rut. "No," she says. "It is not the time."

And then Sheba takes out, from inside the plaiting of her black hair, a golden ring, and hands it to Solomon. He receives it with a gasp. For it resembles in many ways the breastplate of twelve engraved gems worn by the high priests of Israel for the purpose of divination. But it is more concise, more pristine. Four gems only shine from the four sides of the circle, and these, Sheba explains in a whisper so perfect Solomon hardly recalls her speaking, signify writing and numbering (the blue stone), the equality of male and female (the green stone), blood (the red stone), and light (a dull reflecting metal). Solomon bends his head and puts his left hand up to his forehead and eye and lets her gift wash over him like a wind, like a wave, like a dance, like a flame in the night of exile. And he grasps it all perfectly, and constructs many internal equations for himself as to its use. And her power is passed on to him.

"What is the queen of Sheba's given name?" asks King Solomon's secretary and medical expert Joseph ben Barakhya, called Lightning, bending to put a kiss on the forehead of the woman on his sleeping mat.

The first minister of Sheba is taut and conscious in her feathers and jewelry, her hands clasped behind her head. She shrugs away the kiss. But senses no danger from the fellow.

"We really don't have names like that," she says, "but I call her Maqda." With one brown foot she lifts the corner of ben Barakhya's wool throw.

The scribe's eyes sparkle. "That means?" he says, scratching something on the side of a clay pot.

"Mmmm," the minister says, scratching the inside of her elbow. "I think it means Greatness, Great One," she says.

"Yes? Yes?"

"Well," continues the minister, "the woman Sarahil told me it meant 'Great One' and 'leader, guide,' and like that. But she's a Himyarite. There was another in our companionate who had voyaged in her life beyond the sea of pearls to the place where the peacocks breed, and she said that Maqda was a short form of Magadhi. And that Magadhi was a long-gone tribal language, in which there were once sixty-three different ways to say each word, and all so precise and so smooth. But in our language the whole Magadhi tribe and their language have come down to no more than 'the letter *M*.' That's what Maqda means."

The scribe, delighted, offers his guest a liquid delicacy. After a moment he returns from the oven corner with a brew of leaves that has been boiling for days. The minister sits up, crosses her legs, drinks some, and makes a face. But she appreciates the gesture.

"So your people call the queen Maqda," says ben Barakhya happily.

"No," says the minister, "it's her baby name. Almost nobody knows it."

"And you?"

The Sheban minister, glancing around the scribe's modest home, decides to milk the ox a little, and proceeds to tell a long tale about her childhood and youth with the queen of Sheba. She emphasizes the theme of wealth. Minute architectural details. Marble sculpture. Fragrant candles. Gold, silver, brocade, and crystal. Above all, the interesting ceilings. The while she toys with her rings and various bracelets.

"Aha, so you are the queen of Sheba's sister!" declares the scribe, thoroughly pleased.

"Yes. I am her sister." The minister stares at him. "But you have such small families here. Sheba and I had the same seven mothers. The same twelve fathers."

"What—under heaven!" ben Barakhya stammers. "You mean, 'the same mother and father.'"

"No," says the minister. "We don't do it like that."

Existential nausea. "What do you mean, 'We don't do it like that'? You mean . . . you mean . . ."

"Yes, that's what I mean," says the Sheban first minister and priestess, with an impulsive, impatient gesture of her arms. "But what's troubling you?"

The scribe-secretary is in an advanced state of distress. He had noticed, to be sure, and, one might say, taken advantage of, the compliance of this woman. But it was always with the thought that such kind of thing is at best indiscreet. Now it turns out the woman in his chambers (he shudders involuntarily) and the visiting queen herself are universally, celestially! unchaste. They do it in groups. O violation of family purity!

But it is a chance to find out—and perhaps his only chance—"Um, what does your queen do exactly," he asks, a blush creeping over his olive cheeks, under the beard, "with her parade bed? How does she use it? Uh, what's it for?" The man leans against the wall, stung with embarrassment and curiosity.

The minister-priestess laughs pleasantly. "Oh, that's only for special occasions," she says, dimpling.

Joseph is relieved. Still curious. "Like the coronation of a new queen?" he says.

The minister giggles. "No, like the full moon."

Now the scribe feels a sudden urgent need for a trip to the well, perhaps to wash his hands sixty or seventy times. In the meantime, trying hard to remain composed and polite, he has begun to recite hygienic and propitiatory formulae under his breath.

Seeing that he has lost interest in the subject of the queen's given name, the first minister of Sheba makes her toilet slowly and regally, taking in as much as can be had by practiced observation of the medical man's household inventory, and leaves.

IN TOWN

Sheba and her minister walk in the misty Jerusalem rain away from their tent encampment and toward the town, dressed inconspicuously as Israelites. The light spray feels soft on their faces.

"How do you like Jerusalem?" the minister asks, with a conspiratorial smile.

Sheba's pink tongue shows for a second between her teeth. "I like him."

"The two women walk toward the market of the prophets. There, elder women lean in wet ragged dignity against the heavy doorposts of spice shops. With discreet glances the Shebans study the way their robes are wound, and their demeanor, quiet as stones. Whitebearded men squat in groups under overhanging roofs, exchanging tokens. Muddy children race in and out of doors, as husbands and wives conduct their daily business with much speech and worry. The hubbub of loud talk surrounds the foreigners on all side. Thought to be sisters, they are ignored.

"I'm having a good time here too," says the minister. She describes the friends she's made: an Assyrian chariot knight, a Chaldean seer, one of the king's bodyguard . . . she goes on. The queen smiles with amusement.

When the rain suddenly starts to fall hard, the two women turn a narrow corner into the priests' market, and stop under a convenient eave. It is a shop. A man with glasses in front of his eyes is sewing tiny sheets of prayer inside of tiny, square, black leather boxes.

The phylacter smiles as the Shebans brush drops of water off their faces. Noting that they are strangers, he offers malt. The queen accepts. The minister simultaneously refuses. The phylacter shrugs, still smiling, as the minister corrects herself, and accepts. Soon the three are sitting and sipping the hot drink contentedly, as the phylacter's wife stands watching from the doorway of the adjoining apartment.

The women admit to being of the Sheban party, though they avoid saying precisely who they are. The phylacter and his wife and a boy and a girl who poke in have a few questions for them about Sheba, but, like most Israelites, they are rather more interested in explaining their own lives to the visitors.

They tell the women that Solomon is a good king, that the slogan of his administration is "peace and truth."

Sheba laughs delightedly to hear it. The minister regards her with alarm, thinking she'll give herself away. But the craftsman and his family are unsuspicious, and only laugh back.

"The sea cast up its wealth for King Solomon," continues the man.

"Is there anything you *don't* like about him?" suggests the minister.

Sheba puts her hand down on the table and studies her fingers. The phylacter glances at his wife. "He taxes us. No one has ever done that before. He's planning to give away some of our cities. And, most important of all, he shouldn't have married that Egyptian."

"That's right," says the phylacter's wife, still standing in the doorway.

"Why do you say that? Doesn't he love her?" asks Sheba cautiously.

"Oh, far from it," says the phylacter's wife, taking a step forward. "I heard in the market from the porter of a high priest that the king only married the Egyptian because of . . . because . . . well, it had something to do with building the Temple. Something she could give him. Like a very valuable brick, or something like that."

"A brick?" says Sheba.

The phylacter shakes his head to explain his wife. "You must know the Egyptian civilization was old when we were a nation traveling in the desert. It is an impressive place. The Jews didn't really want to leave. And King Solomon still yearns for it in his heart, for its creations, for its achievements. But we are simple people. I sew phylacteries here in the market of the priests because of Moses. I have renounced Egypt. Egypt is corrupt. And this woman whom Solomon son of David married is likewise corrupt."

An awful thought occurs to Sheba. "Do you say that because she is dark?" she asks, in a low voice.

"Not really," says the phylacter, pushing his spectacles up to the top of his head and rubbing his eyes. "Well, you see," he says, "if Solomon were going to marry a dark woman, it would have been better for himself and for the whole nation if he had married your queen of Sheba. Now there's a woman with a wholesome intelligence."

This throws Sheba into a turmoil. She struggles to collect her wits. All she can think of is one of Solomon's witticisms—"Buy the truth and sell it not" he said to her one day, when she asked him about truth in the marketplace.

The minister fills the moment with a bit of a joke, a polite thanks on behalf of the Shebans, and stands up and suggests they have to go. For the rain is over, and goats and children are again sloshing through the cobbled streets. Rising, Sheba tucks a little gold ball into a fold of the phylacter's rough tablecloth. And she and the minister smile, wave, and flee the market of the priests, jumping puddles.

Walking back up the hill to their encampment, Sheba muses about the craftsman's pretty red malt cups.

AN INVITATION

It IS SPRING IN JERUSALEM, BUT NOT FULL spring. The days are still short. The plowman has not yet picked up his metal-tipped goad to move the old oxen in the sowing of the last winter grain.

Sheba is watching for the budding of the almond. Finally it comes. Pink blossoms on a slate-violet trunk. Solomon feels it too. He hears the cooing of the wild birds. He decides he will celebrate with a feast.

He will give Sheba calfside flavored with garlic, and lay the table out with gazelle, partridge, and cuckoo. There will be many wines and a hot and spicy salad of almug leaf. Seedcakes. And olives. He calls Ahishar, Gate of My Brother, to set the royal kitchens in motion. And then he approaches Sheba to give her the invitation.

Solomon takes her down to the underground double throne room, called by some "the secret vault." Its floor is tesselate, slate and gold, its walls hung with dark curtains upon tall pillars, and objects and designs of magical significance stand both behind and before the large figure of a burning bush. The king gestures to the queen to be seated.

"We shall dine tonight in the king's inner chamber," he says.

"I think not."

Solomon grasps the golden arm of his chair. "What do you mean?"

"I know the effect of wine and meat on a man's blood. You will take me by force."

"Is that what you think?" Solomon responds, astonished.

Then between them there comes a long moment of silence. Solomon's blood pounds. Sheba's hormones quicken minutely. The king's invitation and question cut like a sword with two perfect edges through their space-time, and then reach the edge of ours.

Sheba rises precipitously from her chair. She crosses the long room. At the far wall she stops and turns back to Solomon, still on his throne, his elbows on the armrest.

"I will be with you at dinner," she says at last. "But to have you in my bed be for me treason."

"How so?" says Solomon, sitting up, passionately curious. "Are you not a monarch?"

"Just so," replies the woman, kicking a golden incense stand. In Sheba, monarch is virgin."

And silence falls again upon the vault. But this silence is not perfect. A stray wisp of melody wafts in from somewhen through a distant, high, slotted window. Many will later speak of "a little bird" as playing a part in this drama, even going so far as to give that bird species and genus, calling it hoopoe and huppo and hudhud and hodi-hodi and mountain cock and wild cock and cock of the wood and cock of the prairie and lapwing. But we know that birds do not live in our universe; they live in heaven, and experience nothing but emotion, and know nothing but the ascent and descent of angels.

As the meal is being prepared, Solomon dictates to the scribe Joseph ben Barakhya, who is engaged in composing *The Book of the Acts of Solomon:*

"A woman from the pagan seat of empire Sheba has arrived to visit us because of the monopoly we hold in world manufacturing, especially the tin, copper, and iron industries which we have collected from throughout these lands and put under effective marketing control. Her civilization is particularly impressed with our forks and knotted pins, and they have for barter some materials of value to us in our public works.

"Herself, she possesses extraordinary character and qualities. Her understanding is not such as is found in a thousand women, and the clarity of her heart is rare in a hundred men. Of course there is a problem in assaying the precise extent of the woman's wisdom, for she flatters us, and praises our own.

"We are drawing together in friendship. The duration of her stay in Jerusalem has not been specified. But so far the time has passed very pleasantly.

"By her request, we will not impose our will upon her, neither in daily matters, nor in matters of royalty and commerce, nor in the way of a man with a maid. There is perhaps no other woman in the world who could make such a request of us. But this is a queen in truth."

By the light of two candle lamps Sheba speaks with her first minister. "I am succumbing," she admits. "He has pledged he will not take me by force if I take nothing of his. Is this some kind of trick? The old desert nomad's stratagem, perhaps, of serving salt and spicy foods, and denying water? As if I did not understand water down to its very gases and airs, I who am mistress of the great dam. Our mothers understood water long ago, and channeled it and made it work for us. We are such an old people. Solomon's have come so recently up from the desert, so recently out of slavery. I will let him trick me."

"No, I don't think you should."

"I know you don't. But what would the others say? The pythoness, for example, she's so wild. Or the librarian—what has she scribbled down on this scrap of skin for me to remember? hmm, well, I can't make it out."

"But do you really want to do this thing, Maqda? Or does the Monomatapa who hurt you when you were small have a part in it? Do you think to love King Solomon only because Mambo made two scars to run upside of your ankle, and you are no longer allowed in the dance?"

The queen smiles at her companion.

"Well, you are entitled to your opinion. But I do not question whom you love, for good reasons or bad, or whom I myself love. I say we love, after all, like the deer and the leopards of the forest, beyond reasoning. And we do what we need to do."

Maqda blows out the candle.

"Good night, my sister."

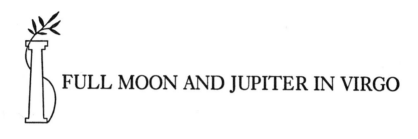

FULL MOON AND JUPITER IN VIRGO

SOLOMON APPROACHES. SHEBA AWAITS IN the adytum, in the holy of holies. Their bodies are smooth and glistening, from the wet rocks, from the sand, from the oils and unguents; all that is as nothing. No web of dust binds them to the earth.

The new moon is past that held a red star in its arms. Solomon approaches, his scarf dangling, rippling, his brown legs moving beneath a dark wool robe. Sheba awaits. The stars have turned.

He arrives then when the moon is at the full, when it is full and red, when its red face shines close by Jupiter, from Zeus, in the precinct of the oak tree judge, true as lightning, conduit of all electricity, in the mansion of the Virgin, celestial nymph, holiest priestess and keeper of the secrets.

Sheba is there for him, Solomon is there. Love falls like dew, like manna, from the immortal heaven, soaking their bodies in sweet timeless forgetting.

Fullmoonnight of the changing of the year betide, the vernal equinox, Solomon has come to Sheba, and Sheba has come for Solomon.

Their limbs entwine atop the coffer of the treaty. Magnetic fields arise and suddenly switch. Demons come to seek the truth and, having no place upon which to rest, fall away, shooting stars. The cherubim supremely approve. The seraphim are vastly engaged. The ofanim are turning, and

113

turning, bring us, even you and me!, to our spots at the tiny golden keyhole.

But we were not meant to see this, and, having seen, we are sworn by all that is true and beautiful to reveal neither the arts nor the sciences that the lover puts to use here tonight in chamber with the beloved.

For to Solomon the world ends this night, and the moon is always full over his kingdom. And the followers of Solomon yet say that this man knew the name of the moon when it has been blessed from every possible side.

Solomon rises to draw the curtain; Sheba is replacing a silver water guglet; they hasten to return to each other.

"Why must we sleep?" he says. "I would have more waking consciousness, more of this honeyed life."

Sheba consoles him with a story. "When the sun went down for the first time," she says, "our ancestor was terrified. Nothing had sex then. There was only one of everything. And there was not even the twoness of eyes, ears, hands. How was our parent to know there would ever be light again? Everything had happened for the first time, and once only." She tickles his toes.

"Go on," says the king.

"Consider, then, the feeling of the first sunrise. Night had turned back into day: eureka! It was a twoness, an amazement, a very, very extremely good thing."

"Indeed."

"So our ancestor murdered the unicorn—you know, the one-horned horse?—because it was the creature of oneness, the creature that most recalled the terror of the apocalypse." She laughs.

"Why do you laugh?"

"In relief. I remember the fear. But I am sad for the unicorn. In the place of immortality nothing was replaceable. That was the last we shall know of the perfection of the beasts. Then was love created for our parent, for play and recreation, for being and manifestation. And much later came the end of immortality and the beginning of pain for the creatures of the enclosed place . . . but that you know."

114

"I know nothing but you."

Sheba is touched. "And I know Solomon, king in Jerusalem, lord of that holy hill where the unicorn was slaughtered that we might sleep without dread."

Then the king kisses Sheba's mouth and closes his eyes for a nap before they will wake to begin lovemaking again. And as he sleeps he dreams of the men who will judge him in future times: men in lax and effeminate cities, who will wear black and dispute till the morning whether he, Solomon, be damned or blessed.

And Sheba sleeps too, and dreams of infinitely ringing ankle bells, and of the fragrances of travelers crossing the desert.

And love, that is her god, that is his devil, emanates in a fine, fine mist from a priest's hut, from a striped Sheban tent, from a granite and limestone Temple too intricately perfect to survive crude history, till it reaches the nooks and crannies of monks' brains bending over golden-lettered manuscripts and freezes again into stone on the greatest cathedrals.

Then, after a while, Solomon and Sheba retire to the great parade bed throne that he has built as a surprise for her, modeled after the secret-most treasure of her realm. Spacious as a field, its hills and valleys of silk make for them a place of indefinite length, a universe of two, and there they are even now making love. Bloom and poetry and spectacle bespangle its corners, in its center runs a meadow brook, and by the side of that brook they lie.

Some say death awaits them there.

But, no. What is death but a glove turned inside out, a dimension close but impossible? Drunk on the elixir of pleasure they hang beyond and outside of time. The long slow shutting of an eyelid cancels out all unpleasantness. Sheba touches Solomon, and his hand is to her. Clothes fall away from their bodies as if the material itself has volition, the weight of gravity. No impulse of haste or uncertainty troubles the motionless mutual circling of the poles. Entirely without will, woman and man are one animal. Together they descend backward through the generations . . . to the primordial Pair, in a cave of fire and fear. And there, as They, they know at last

115

their ringing unitedness and their separateness true unto the unbearable. And into their two bodies is burnt the immutable connection between pleasure and pain. What do we know, really? Except that, since the world was created, man knew woman and woman man, and their love and their death alike were a terror.

In bed with him, Sheba learns to speak the king's language, and the terms of his ways and gods; and he learns to speak the soft tongues of the woman tribes telling of love so ineffable it flickers on the winds of ages.

"Let him love me with the weapons of his mouth."

"Thy breasts are better than wine."

"The smells of your oils are good."

"I am a seeker, O ye daughters of Jerusalem. Look not upon me, because I am incendiary. My mother's sons would stab me in the throat, but I bear no wound, only a grudge. In the grove of sacred harlotry I have not stayed."

"You pasture me, but I have imagined you a horse in pharoah's chariots!"

"Tell me, O thou whom my soul loveth, where do you fight, where do you study? Should I instigate something at high noon in the pastures of your friends?"

 A JUDGMENT

AT DAWN THEY WAKE IN LANGUOR AMONG the emblems of their power. Storehouses of gold dust to the millions of dollars. There is no coin in the days of the Temple, but there are ingots and circlets and bricks of gold; stores of wood and iron chariots for war trimmed in gold and idols for the Phoenician ships: gold; and gold color shiny beaten utensils for the home. And in beautiful carved chests long lengths of the soft white materials to wrap around the body, to catch the morning.

But they are still suffused with love, and most aware of where they have intersected.

"I thought the world would end," Sheba whispers, brushing her hair.

"O! Let us try again!"

That day Sheba stays with Solomon as he sits in the judgment seat, watching him scatter away evil with his glance. She applauds him, and he expands in her approval.

"You are the daughter of the voice," he whispers to her. "My judgments if they are correct come through you. Where you are is the center, the nucleus, of the world."

Halfway through the day Sheba and Solomon hear the case of the two nursing mothers. The queen longs to adjudicate it herself, to take the women by the shoulders and comfort them, to sit them down with carved fruit and qat, to smoke and relax and let the truth of their tale emerge.

Solomon's approach is entirely different. He looks at the baby both women claim as their own. He pushes back his crown and scratches his neck when they speak of the second babe, who died in the night. And then, to the shock of the priests, pages, slaves, scribes, and gawkers filling the hall of judgment, he bursts from his chair and brandishes a sword over the head of the squalling infant. "Divide the difference!" some think they hear him say.

"No!" cries Sheba. And she too jumps to her feet, and flings her arms upon Solomon's, staying the hilt of the sword with her fists.

One of the mothers screams and thrusts the baby at the woman she was contesting a moment before, pleading for mercy. Solomon at once declares this woman to be the rightful mother, and awards her the child. The crowd in the gallery goes wild; enthusiastic scribes record the scene furiously. "Wisdom," is whispered round, as a shamefaced woman and a timid mother dandling a crying infant exit the court and other litigants quickly take their place. Sheba decides she will step out for a breath of air.

"Something you love will be divided, Solomon," she murmurs as she leaves.

The king makes a note to ask her what she means, but somehow that long day it slips his mind.

Late in the afternoon, inside a striped tent in the Sheban encampment, Sheba gives Solomon to drink from the goblet that is a single piece of green stone. He quaffs the wine eagerly, vowing love with his eyes.

"Why do you tax your subjects, Solomon?" she asks him. "Why do you give your cities away? Why did you marry the Egyptian?"

Incense curls up from a Sheban censer: cobra-headed, five tears surrounding a disc. The scent is that they call from Achaea to China "the true scent," and associate with their gods.

Solomon clears his throat to speak about the Temple. A Temple to the Without-Ending, to be made of the costliest stuffs according to the most divine work-plan. How in David's time there was a spontaneous outpouring of gifts from the people into the royal treasury, which supported the work. But how now the work is harder and slower, and the share of the costs must be enforced among the many.

The cities, he tells her, he is obligated to give to King Hiram of Tyre in partial repayment for the immense wealth of material, workmen, and know-how that that king has provided.

And he married the Egyptian, he says (after a moment of hesitation), "because I was under the delusion that the great secrets of measurement, design, and engineering resided with the Egyptian patrimony, and could be sold with its daughters."

Sheba nods. She is familiar with the works of Egypt. But that woman is a lazy, drowsy cat. "How did you find her?" she asks.

Now it is for Solomon to look into Sheba's eyes and search there for something deeper than curiosity. But he sees only that self-sufficient intelligence he finds so compelling, her spiritual virginity. So he reins back his feelings.

"I found that she had lost touch with the cosmogony from which her sciences sprang, and that she interested herself, if at all, only in trivia and self-referential consistency. There was nothing for me there."

"And the Temple rose without the help of Egypt, then?" she continues, for the work is evident all around.

And the king takes her hand and holds it tightly, and says, "I learned from King Hiram of an architect and of others who were educated in the hidden academies. He told me much. His workmen showed me much. I put the very most ancient men of Egypt to work. Now I know a great deal that my father did not, when he began this work. And you, my darling, I feel you, too, will have something to teach me of this matter before the final consecration of the holy places is done."

When this day is past and darkness descends again, Solomon stands on the high fourth-storey parapet of the treasure house and sees that the stars are real. He has purged himself of his mother and boyhood. He has come out from under the wonderful canopy of artifice fashioned by the pharaoh's daughter's men. Free, as if from an old husk, he stands and breathes the evening air and feels his life moving along the way. The sky swings slow around. Now is very long. The lines of configuration are all significant, and divination is thick in the air, real as

119

flesh. For the first time in his life Solomon sees his dream of a Temple as completely real.

And Solomon sees Sheba as a high priestess seated between the two pillars of the left- and the right-hand ways, guarding with her person and her being the third way, between. He aspires to her way, to approach her endlessly; and, at his side, she aspires to him.

AN ARAB TALE

An Arab caravaneer sits sipping on a nargileh in the oasis at Tabuk, telling a story to his blood brothers and blood cousins that they will be calm, and resist the desire to go out on raiding. It comes to him from a kahin diviner of their acquaintance who has been to Jerusalem and come back with a tale for all the desert; and it shall be embellished, and made local, and recited tonight above the gentle lowing of the camels, and again tomorrow.

"It seems," says the Arab, "that there was a pretender to the throne of prophesy by the name of Moshailama, and a challenger to him, one Shedja the Perfect, prophetess of a numerous tribe. They had already heard speak of one another when this woman sent Moshailama a letter suggesting a meeting, with their disciples present, for mutual examination and discussion—to determine whether she were truer prophet than he. Her messenger was accompanied by an army of disciples on horses; Moshailama was dismayed. But an elder man told him how to trick her."

Here the Arab inhales deeply on the bubbling water-pipe and pauses. The group around him urges him vehemently to continue, especially the younger boys.

"Outside the city Moshailama erected a tent in which to greet Shedja, made of colored brocade and silk. And this he filled, so that none might escape, with the scents of amber and musk and rose and orange blossom and jonquil and jasmine and hyacinth and carnation and, burning in gold censers, green aloe and ambergris and benzoin. And perhaps some other plants as well.

"And when Shedja entered this place, where Moshailama had enthroned himself, to engage him in conversation, the perfumed vapor was dense enough to impregnate the water in their cups. Her bones relaxed and she lost her presence of mind in delight. Then did Moshailama take possession of the female prophet—on her back, on all fours, and kneeling as in prayer with her crupper in the air—for in all ways did she desire it. And he enjoyed her also to the extent of granting her request for marriage.

"Then Moshailama was freed of the embarrassment caused to him by the excellent and powerful Shedja the Perfect and her army. Though her people never did recognize any prophet but herself."

He stops.

A boy says, "What happened to Moshailama?"

"He was killed by a Negro," says the caravaneer, and exits smoothly, with swirling skirts, to walk behind a palm and relieve himself.

BOOK THE FOURTH
THE MASONS

OUT OF EGYPT

THE TECHNICAL KNOWLEDGE BY WHICH the pyramids had been built fifteen hundred or more years earlier still inhered, at the time of Solomon, in the workings and teachings of the brotherhood of builders. Rich and glorious in their own traditions, the masons were a breed near invisible to all others. Some would say they did their most superlative work for all time near the delta of the Nile. But they had not remained within pharaonic Egypt.

Orders had come down that were intolerable. They were called upon to perform acts for political reasons they could not abide. Of course some acquiesced, and stayed on, for a few crumbs and a place to rest. Here is such a straggler mason: He is throwing a statue down from its base. He is hacking out its eyes. He is striking the cobra from its brow. He is splintering it, with hammer, chisel, and maul. He is chipping out some name wherever it appears; he is substituting other names. But he has his pride—he will leave it for vandals and thieves to pull off a monarch's nose.

By far the greater number of the sacred builders, later called *hierolatomi*, were unbound spirits, who fled the unjust and immoral regimes. When the priests became too powerful in the old high place of On, city of Re, and set themselves up over the practical geometers, the masons slowly but thoroughly abandoned the city. They rowed to all ports of the Great Sea. They scattered overland with their families in horse carts. They moved like nomads in small communes, never risking the visibility of a caravan. They resembled tinkers and smiths, with their tools and aprons. Sometimes they put the T-shaped cross on their foreheads as a sign for "god" and "iron." Until finally On, ancient city of the sun, was nothing more than an obelisk in a wheatfield, the dimmest memory, whose wise men had gone to Alexandria, whose stones had been carried to Cairo.

Up the coastline in Phoenicia, where the alphabet was born, and literacy had soared in a rush, they found a more favorable climate for their work. In Tyre they labored for Maviael, who pioneered in the uses of cedar. Under Jabal they constructed two pillars for a temple of Hercules, one of gold and one of emerald. Much later they obliged a willful boy-king and built the island city up into a peninsula. They journeyed out from the mother city to Carthage, and from Carthage across the Great Sea the short way to Sicily; and all the time they preserved faithfully the secrets of stone, brick, and engraving, and of care of the dead.

They settled in the holy land as well, divided into two parties. Followers of Father-King settled in Gaza, the place of treasure. And followers of Righteous-King settled in Salem, the place of peace.

At the time of Solomon, brother masons usually wore beards but no mustaches, and their wives were beautiful and worked through childbirth. Flowers and grain were holy to them, and also the right angle, and the circle compass that draws a straight line on a sphere, and also the four-string lyre, and a certain star. Bending to elbow height, they surveyed the land wherever destiny placed them. Plumb stone fell from A-square, and they lived by geometry. Among them it could never be forgotten how to erect colossal statues with mirror-smooth surfaces out of the hardest rock.

They knew their tools and their materials, and they knew the uses of silence. Thus, though they were all around him in the lands of Canaan and Syria when Solomon was anointed king, he did not, truly speaking, know of them until introduced into their order by Hiram king of Tyre.

*   *   *

126

Now they had gathered again. Masons and carpenters, stonesquarers, hewers of wood, drawers of water, philosophers, sawers of the underground lime, smelters of bronze, architects, smiths in silver and gold, apprentices, journeymen, astronomers, masters—skilled craftsmen and artists in the thirty-nine kinds of sacred work—they swung their tanned and muscled arms of many shades, throughout the land of Canaan from the Great Sea across the hills to Jerusalem, and on beyond, to the plains of the Jordan, and to Jericho, hard upon the Salt Sea; and in all these places they builded the Temple, their energies focused on Temple mountain. Disciples of Re at On and of Memphian Ptah, they knew that no limit could be set to art, that no craftsman was fully master of his craft. Yet they felt in their arms, and their legs, and their sweat, that this assignment from Solomon and Hiram was worthy of the brotherhood. And their wives and little children felt so too, and pridefully loved them when a month's work was done and a shift returned home.

Daily the felled trees of Lebanon arrived at the western port: beautiful conifers, resilient and waterproof. Woodmen had cut down the evergreens far from the Temple site, and carpenters smoothed and finished the long logs into boards for the walls and floors of the high houses at sites also far distant. And this was because Solomon did not consider it good to have the loud sound of iron tools in the near workings. Iron was the hand of war; merely to remember and consider it caused a shameful weakening in the belly.

Across the Jordan on the eastern plains, the freemasons cast a bronze water-dish for the Temple court so big that they first cast twelve bronze oxen, each larger than a man, to support it. Before the architect called Hiram poured the tons of burning metal into these huge molds, he spoke among the Chaldeans and the Gibeonites, and some of the old Egyptians as well, who knew the heavenly bodies and the movements in sky and atmosphere, to determine the most auspicious moment for the task. A crack in a mold, of ox or "molten sea," and thousands could die, in the horrible lava of artifice. The starry men recommended a certain moonless night. That evening the flaming red-orange liquid metal lit up the sky, and women saw it seventy-five miles away in Gilead. And the work was done smoothly.

In the Temple precincts white stones as heavy as a thousand men were set into immaculate row upon row with an effortlessness known only to the masons, that eluded the nation's wisdom. The engineering was brilliant, supernatural. Yet the builders were human men: their torsos hard with work and good pace, short skirts around their lean hips. If a small Judaean boy were to wander up and ask them how they finished off the rock (the implacable granite!) so cleanly (to within a knife's edge!) and lifted it (and the sun-dried limestone, and the massive marble), not having seen them do it—like as not a freemason would laugh and rumple the child's hair and tell him a woodpecker had dropped some seeds into a crevasse in the rock which, growing and expanding, had split it.

Now Solomon son of David was called grand master of the work when the Temple in Jerusalem was being builded, for he had commissioned it and contracted for it and (some said) played a part in its design. Since Hiram king of Tyre controlled the overseas sources of wealth that made the work possible, and at least half of the work force, he was called a grand master of the work as well. And "the other Hiram" of Tyre, the architect, a descendant of the tribes of Dan and Naphtali, was the third of the grand masters.

All these three men came together occasionally to discuss the business of the Temple building, meeting in the spot that would when it was finished be the holiest in the whole IHVHist complex, insofar as mere space could be holy. Behind the spreading gold wings of the two sacred angels, the highest of the Judaean high priests would, much later, commune with the most high God in elaborate ceremonies of fire and water and cattle death and, inspired by the tribes' highest symbols, in the sight of the word . . . might utter oracles of guidance.

But on a daily basis it was mostly Hiram the architect who spent time in the holy of holies. If someone could have observed him alone there, one would have seen only a thoughtful, long-haired man pondering measurements made on scraps of different materials and sketching with a stylus on a wax-covered drawing board. Once in a great while he smoked a small cheroot, then crushed and pulverized it minutely, as if in anger.

Hiram was a liberal. He was loyal by choice to both kings, Hiram and Solomon, but he valued as well his own interests of life and happiness. It concerned him that there were Edomite slaves mining the Arabah under poor conditions in the southern part of Solomon's kingdom, but, except in polite conversation with the monarch, he wasn't going to do anything about it. His watchwords were tolerance, resistance, endurance.

And he was a cosmopolitan. He considered himself a cousin to all races. He looked to the design of Egypt, the music of the black men beyond the Nile, the literature of golden Babylonia. He knew that in the lands past Sheba there were struggles between the chiefs of the ceremony of innocence and the chiefs of the axen bloodbath; and he knew which side he was on. Once he had met a seven-foot-tall Watusi, and he had been impressed by the health and sanity of that man's ways.

And Hiram had done good work in Tyre. But Hiram's preeminence in the building of Solomon's Temple was not due to his reputation. Nor had it been granted by his patron, the king of Tyre. It had come to him by his merit, on a specific day. On the morning that the foundation stone for the building was being laid, and the masons were still massing from all the lands of their exile, Hiram the architect drew a diagram on his trestle board of a certain three-sided figure, and he observed that the squares drawn on the short sides summed up exactly equal to the square drawn on the longest side: and he cried out "Eureka!" And Solomon appreciated this accomplishment, and appointed him Grand Architect of Jerusalem.

Some among the masons said that this Hiram, son of the widow woman, was an artist wiser than the world had ever seen. Others argued, as they sat down to lunch on a grassy knoll between the thistle and the almond, that the work of the men of a hundred nationalities was the key; and that unless each one of these men—every last one—felt and continued to feel that his agreement was sacred, they could do nothing; but so long as

129

the decision to cooperate was made again and again every morning by every man, then the boundaries of their work would continue to amplify.

Many nations were in the work force. Twelve tribes of Hebrews. The ancient Amorites, brothers to the Hebrews. The Hivites who taught the Hittites to write. The bellicose Hittites, in their high cone hats. Hurrians out of the northern mountains. Jebusite kin of both Amorite and Hivite. In largest numbers were the pharaoh's men, from Egypt, the dowry of Solomon, who were old and not strong; and King Hiram's Phoenicians, the backbone of the force. Among these last the men of Byblos led the rest, being most adept in their crafts as well as superior in philosophy and geometry —though they referred to themselves modestly as "stonesquarers."

There was, however, certain labor that the masons did not do. As Hiram and many of the others were aware, no free man worked in the iron and copper mines of the Arabah. This wet, dirty, and very dangerous job was done by slaves of the region, female and male. Mostly Edomites, they bore their oppression by telling each other that their lot was not so bad as that of the Egyptian slave miners in Nubia, where for every two who dug up the gold, one died of thirst. And they liked to speak among themselves also of Hadad, the native prince, who would return one day and save them, and revenge the destruction of his people.

THE PHARAOH'S DAUGHTER'S PLAN

SOMETHING IN THE LANGUID AIR OF
Jerusalem summer stirred the pharaoh's daughter. She knew
that the moon and the three planets of Osis, Osir, and their
child had moved into the constellation of hippopotamus with
crocodile on its back, and she expected a certain urgency, or
intensity, of personal relations, perhaps a gradually complicat-
ing situation brought to a decision point.

I shall entertain Sheba, she thought.

In rooms behind and below her bower in the Mount Zion
suburb, servants bustled to keep Solomon's wife comfortable
with imported treats—frying papyrus stalk, salting fish, setting
up blue and white blossoms in vases with special clamps to hold
them; none heard her now, speaking to herself, nor knew the
plan forming in her mind.

Soon after, Sheba came to the queen's pavilion to visit with
the younger woman. She was motivated by curiosity, and
affected a facade of friendliness. But both had the same dim,
fierce sense of mortal rivalry.

The Egyptian took an infinitesimal sip of barley wine and
waved a breath of narcotic scent toward her nose. She waved
Sheba into a low chair. Then she began to speak of musical
instruments. At first Sheba paid no attention, having no
expertise in the matter and not recognizing many of the words
the Egyptian was using for situations arising in the composition
of music and in its playing.

131

She spoke of the nose flute and the longer pipe and the pipe with more holes and the double flute; and of the multiple pipes and the small hand drum and the hand drum with bells called the drum of Moses' sister or tambourine; and of the double-sided drum, and the wooden castanets; and of the golden flute, the single-string mandola with wood plectrum, the seven-string hand harp of various sizes, and the lyre; and of the eleven-, thirteen-, or fourteen-string standing harp; and of the metal hand rattle.

That one I know, thought Sheba, for the sistrum with discs on vertical rods was used in her country. But she wondered why the pharaoh-queen was going at such length. What does she want of me? Sheba looked at her broad, squarely boned face and the hair falling down straight and thick around her ears. Almost as if she could read Sheba's mind, when the pharaoh-queen observed she was being observed, she greatly increased the animation of her mouth and hands (though her eyes were stolid and opaque as stone); her intention was to ward off any bad emanations from the Sheban. And she stepped up her discourse, already thick with esotericisms, even further.

"The circle tambourine and the straight-sided tambourine," she began, and held forth on their uses, finishing with a description and analysis of the closed tambourine with parchment, or darabukka. Then she went into the copper drum and the double drum. The Hathor-headed sistrum versus the flower-petal sistrum of the monotheists, and both of these compared with the goddess-and-flower combination sistrum. Military trumpet with long thin tube, and short-tube trumpet. Arm-long tenor flute. Double pipes in reed case. Semitic lyre with five, six, seven, eight, ten, thirteen, or eighteen strings. Bow harp with double strings. Syrian lute with long straight stem and tassels. Lute harp, with curved neck and bowl. The Mesopotamian trigon, or right-angled treble harp.

Despite herself, Sheba was impressed. She appreciated the crowd of sounds the queen of Israel had brought to her loveless throne from the royal house of Egypt. And she felt some sympathy for this wife of Solomon, realizing now how profound was her unwilling displacement from the civilization she loved.

She had no questions to ask on the subject of the woman's monologue. But she admired her fluency.

Nor could they speak of personal relations, for fate had placed Solomon of Israel right in each other's blind spot. So Sheba took the lead in the conversation, and introduced a topic of public interest.

"Solomon is building a great monument," said Sheba, "don't you think?"

This was exactly what the pharaoh-queen wanted to hear. Sheba stating her needs. She would fulfill Sheba's need. And then Sheba would be ripe to fulfill hers, the Egyptian's own, and she would get a large boon at a small price.

"Be frank with me," smiled the Egyptian shrewdly, "and I will tell you some things about the pyramids that Solomon has always wanted to know, and that I have never told him."

This sounds interesting, thought Sheba.

And the Egyptian delivered herself of a second extraordinary speech for the queen of Sheba. All the musical instruments she had named, and knew so well, sounded in her mind as silent accompaniment, skillfully blended into an archetypal euphony; and her words themselves were heavy and carved, mysterious and sacerdotal as hieroglyphics. And Sheba listened with her chin on her fist to the wisdom of her sister of the Nile.

"The inventor of building with hewn stone was Imhotep, a black African," the Egyptian said, "also called by the Thebaid 'the father of medicine.' In the language of the High Mountain River, a civilization great at that early time as many generations ago as there are years in a man's life, the name of Imhotep was called Mahatapas, which means to them Great Sacrifice, or Penance. By this they signified what we would call now Self-Torture. The king served by Imhotep we call Djosher. And this Djosher was a round-faced Mongol who wore the fez crown of the high Tibetan plateau. In his birth lands far to the east there had also been such a one as this African Mahatapas who had willingly cut down his own life finger by finger in order to increase the wisdom of the king. There they called the willing fire sacrifice 'Agni.' And to this day, in the east, all words for terrible wisdom have this sound of 'gn' in them.

"But I speak of Imhotep of the long river, who cut back his own life, inch by inch. . . . His was a work of supreme devotion, and of loyalty to a foreign king he conceded to be divine. Each new height of suffering understanding that he reached came forth spurting, like a fountain of blood, which he crystallized in his wisdom and transformed into a book of medicine. And this knowledge that he bought with his life he established in a visible structure, an architecture the world had never seen the like of, and that his masons to this day call the 'pyramid.'

"This was the first of the ten-finger temples built later with so much sorrow and care by the kings of the double royal house in the black land. It was a museum and a laboratory and an academy, and the wisdom that passed between voices and ears during the work on its stages was ultimate. But hawk and falcon and tiger and crocodile do not reign immortal in Cheme. They die. And their place is taken by the winged rodent and the gecko lizard. And so, too, the great secret knowledge of the slowly dying Imhotep could not after all be preserved for man, except in bare outline and shadow. Without his scribe and companion we would not know even this. Much is lost. The builders preserved the art of hewing and polishing the big stones, and some of the science of aligning them best to master the spaces and times of the planet. They continued to build. But there was too much to record—even with a writing tool as long as a man's body—and so we have forgotten the better part. Much of what was built afterward was stone and brick only, and without a soul."

Sheba lifted her cup of barley wine. She told the pharaoh-woman of the dam at Marib, whose deeper significance—the control of passion and its sublimation—was remembered even after the secrets of its masonry had been forgot. But her defenses were too soon relaxed.

For a poison fire was burning in the Egyptian. That tattletale of a little Tyrian princess, visiting in Jerusalem with her father, had told a eunuch, who told a cook in the Egyptian apartments, who told the pharaonic hairdresser, who told the queen of Israel: that Solomon and Sheba had made love on the altar of the Temple. Worst of all, the message had come to the

Egyptian queen with some of its joy still intact; in another lifetime, in another place, in Sheba perhaps, the young girl might have said, "How lucky am I, to be a priestess of the first temple, and an initiate of the adytum, where even now the solemn and sacred ceremony of blessing is being performed!" And that could not be forgiven.

Now the keynote of Egyptian revenge-magic was understood by the queen, Solomon's great wife, and it was this: that to produce the best effect by words of power one must utter them in a certain tone of voice, at a certain rate, at a certain time of day or night, with appropriate gestures or ceremonies. . . . All this she had taken into account, from the first breath of her invitation through all the talk of harps and sistra, in the sip of the barley wine and the pleasant scent of the intoxicant. At last Sheba had been perfectly prepared.

And the pharaoh-princess mentioned . . . Hiram.

THE PASSWORDS CHANGE

W<small>AS IT IN</small> E<small>DOM,</small> <small>THEN,</small> <small>THAT THE TROU-</small>
ble started? Among the red men, their skins like clay, who had
been tricked by Jacob and massacred by David's general Joab?
Did the freemasons see the sorrow of the slaves and wish to
help them?

For from somewhere, discreet as a wind at night, a dissatis-
faction arose among the builders and spread throughout the
ranks.

The overseer Jeroboam put it about that Solomon was not
planning the work in the best interests of the people. To
sweeten his hand among the men, he demanded increased
wages and more rapid promotions.

Hiram, chief architect and paymaster, was the most exposed
of the grand masters, and he felt the stirrings first.

One restless evening before the Sabbath day, when the
weekly wage was being distributed in the outer chamber of the
Temple under construction, the first untoward event occurred.
Ordinarily the different pay grades of workmen announced to
the paymaster at what level they worked, and were paid
accordingly. To keep things square, the ranks were specified in
code. Usually the burden bearers and apprentices said, "servitude," and the journeymen masons and carpenters and casters
said, "workers' pool," and the overseers said, "the way." And
in the old Semitic tongue all these three phrases sounded
almost exactly alike, but for an accent or inflection.

But tonight some seemed to be slurring their passwords. Or were they declaring something altogether different? This new word, that meant "kernel" and "crux" and "spike," and sounded so very much like the other words—*shibboleth*—what did they mean by it? Was it an accident of speech? A dialect? Or was it, as Hiram suddenly thought in horror, that there were those from among the apprentices and journeymen whose sense of grievance, at some real injustice or imagined slight, had already reached an advanced state? That they sweated and breathed immediate change? That they longed to take up their tools of work in the cause of war? Perhaps Jeroboam knew. But first, Hiram went to tell Solomon.

When King Hiram got wind of the business with the passwords he hurried down from Tyre. From long experience with temple building, with statues of gods that had to be chained in place to prevent their being spirited away by rival forces, he knew that worker unrest was a signally bad omen. He hated even to speak of it.

King Hiram and King Solomon met in a cave beneath Jerusalem, whence great slabs of wet lime had been removed. Solomon indicated that they should wait for the other Hiram, without whom a meeting of the grand masters could not take place. But King Hiram waved a hand toward some three armed men, his servants, who stood in the light at the entranceway of the long cave. There was a fine point of masonic lore here that Solomon did not know. "For a meeting of craftsmen only five persons are necessary," said Hiram brusquely, "we two grand masters, and they three fellow crafts."

Solomon did not challenge the king of Tyre. He was disturbed. He paced up and down in the gloom. "Last time this happened it was blamed on the Ephraimites," he said. "They always pronounce *s, sh.*"

King Hiram said he understood the general nature of the problem, but had no details.

"'Siboloth' is what the apprentices usually say to get their wage," said Solomon. "Meaning servitude. And the journeymen say 'sibboleth,' for workers' pool. And the overseers say something similar."

"Yes?"

"Yes, and since the new moon of this month, more and more of the men have been saying 'shibboleth.'"

"Meaning?"

"Current of the river, eddy, vortex; kernel; spike."

"Say that word again—?" requested Hiram.

"Shibboleth."

"Ah, yes. I didn't hear you right. In Phoenician the spike refers to Spica, the star, the bright star in the High Priestess— you call her the Virgin? Do you suppose our men have something they want to say abour your visiting queen or her priestesses?"

"Oh, no, impossible," said Solomon roughly, and commenced to pace again, with long strides.

But King Hiram was skeptical. "Are you ready for some difficult advice?" he said. Solomon nodded but did not stop pacing. "All right, then. I say your Temple will abort unless we deliver by the knife. The brothers are unhappy. I have seen the signs many times before."

"What are you saying?" said Solomon, looking at him hard.

Hiram smiled an awful smile. "It is hard to say in Hebrew. It sounds better in Phoenician. And very soft indeed in some tongues I might mention. Er, that is, I mean to say: your work can be protected with the sacrifice of a life. Give the masons the queen of Sheba."

"Oh, my God, no!"

"By the gods," said King Hiram of Tyre. "Perhaps."

And the two strolled the length of the cave toward Jericho, discussing the unthinkable idea. "You recoil," said Hiram, "because your tribes are warriors. You have bought collective human sacrifice and sold representative individual redemption. I know, it doesn't translate well."

He continued. "We Phoenicians are not warriors. We are linguists, merchants, and boatmen. Trust me on this. The older gods, the goddesses, all the great ones that not even our friend Hiram understands fully though he deals with them

139

every day, the divinities and judges and powers—these see more in heaven and earth than your brazenly triumphant individuality. I know. Trust me."

Night fell sudden and hot, and the Temple was almost finished.

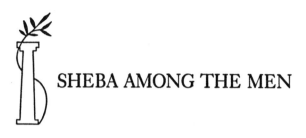

SHEBA AMONG THE MEN

THE BUILDERS' TROUBLE CONTINUED TO brew. Every day workers begged leave on grounds of illness. It was said that the overseer Jeroboam was calling meetings in secret and encouraging the men to air their grievances.

So Solomon took his priestess Sheba, his love queen, out to survey the progress of the masonry in his company. He told her he thought the radiance of her femininity would affect the builders and make them whole and tranquil.

On Solomon's arm, Sheba walked among the masons, curious and candid, relishing a thrill few women ever know: to be alone among thousands, and thousands, of men. They hailed and cheered her from every side, and spoke to her with polite interest. Along the western flank of the steps that encircled the inner courtyard were gathered the artisans in gold, sitting, kneeling, standing, or walking about, and all completing various tasks. One man she noticed was polishing a fifteen-branched candelabrum: a token, Solomon told her, of the Egyptian five and the masonic three. Men in striped kilts handled the innumerable drinking service. An old woman called Bird was sewing a curtain blue as the twilight sky.

Sheba was not so excited by the work in precious metals, for there was much of it in her own land. Indeed, her arrival in Jerusalem bearing six tons of fine gold had had a noticeable effect on the work. It had been decided by Solomon, Hiram, and Hiram (always deferring to the late king's bequest and legacy) that the Sheban gold should plate the timber all around: floor, walls, ceiling, doors; inside and out; so that the house of the unnameable Lord might shine like a sun. The peaceful olive, the sovereign cedar, the resurrect cypress—all had been covered with the gold of Sheba.

And there it stood now, nearly finished, in the focal point of the great squared-off, marble-paved, granite summit of the mountain, in the inviting center of eight parallel sets of gates and two wide, concentric open courtyards. Amid rows of priestly housing, the Temple rose like a dream, brilliant and mysterious, iridescent in the distance, light and dark reflecting in hazy vertical stripes all around its circumference. Unlike the palaces of Sheba, it tended to the square. But it was not square; there was some trickery about the sides, and something audacious and strange about its shape. From the foundation unto the spreading of the roof it rose ever wider, like an upside-down pyramid. It was made of wood and stone and sapphire, and of silver, lime, and ivory, and of an alabaster of transparent refulgence, and of gold.

As the queen and Solomon walked slowly across the court-yards full of workmen and scaffolding, she noticed their spirit, and their eyes, and their stance. And she thought also about the other kinds of crowds that might fill this high, walled-in, welcoming space. She thought of the mass that had come to see her here during the riddling. And she thought of the gatherings that would come to celebrate the seasonal plantings and harvestings, fresh-bathed, exuberant, and full of themselves, drawn only by the geometric gravity of this spot. She let go of the king's arm, then, thinking warm thoughts toward the women and children of Judaea, and they passed between the immense fire altar and the immense water basin.

And when the king and queen had come at last to the front of the Temple, stepping one step up to the stately porch she remembered from the many mornings of questioning here, something new and very large commanded her attention. The late morning sun was beaming hot on the copper brass bronze sides of the Standing Pair, and these reflected back a dazzling orange-brown gold. As Solomon beside her basked in pride, his hand on her mantle, Sheba lifted her face to them and they rose five or six times the height of a man straight upward, and beyond that, more than another height of a man, rounded into a grand pattern she liked even before she had closely seen or been told of it. There, so high the blazing Oriental sun was in her eyes, she could make out a fabulous metal netting, fluid as lace, which caught in its ethereal folds the fruit bursting with seed and the pale chaste flower.

This I shall have in Axum, thought Sheba.

Then, from between the pillars, Sheba turned to survey the entire threshing floor of Araunah, now transformed into a triple shrine, splendid and superb. Someone, architect or stonemason, had played reckless, wonderful magic with the sun and air of these holy mountains. The monuments were huge and spacious, and widening toward the roof they made one think of soaring toward a widening heaven. Sixty pillars around the sides of the Temple house in rows that grew progressively taller alternated darkness and light with a shimmer, and made the holy place cool and thoughtful as a crystalline forest. Seen from a distance it was a mass; but here the structure seemed all openwork. It was not her original mission or idea or intention to become involved with such as engineering. The great round dam in her land had been built so long before that the miracle of work was taken for granted. But she trusted her feelings, and she was feeling this space with her quietest inward being. All the differentness of the thousands of men surrounding her and Solomon, many with their eyes on her, flowed into the queen of Sheba like a burning current. From deep inside the core of the Temple there suddenly stepped forth Hiram.

Hiram's body was broad at the shoulders and narrow at the hips. To look at him one would say his parents had conceived him while listening to a lyre. His hand was steady; whatever he gripped (or only touched with the point of his stylus) he aligned correctly. Around his large head his hair fell in lovelocks to his neck, a thick profusion of fine ringlets dark in the shade but fair on the sunlit porch. This head he held a little stiffly now as he beheld Sheba and was introduced to her for the first time (for he had been far from the royal couple during the riddling), but he seemed to listen very well, and to intercept something invisible she was sending out.

Sheba felt a rush of confusion. She hardly looked at the man. She looked at the king looking at him. Solomon had a point of pink in his cheek. But Hiram was having none of that. He fended off Solomon's flushed glance with subtle gestures and modulated speech, and did not overreact. Like Sheba, he did not believe in Solomon's devil. He spoke to the king with unmistakable respect.

Nearly overwhelmed, Sheba's reason struggled to order her experience. These two men, together, unnerved her more than thousands gazing from all around. As they spoke of trowel and book, Sheba heard and saw angels flying out of their mouths, she saw worlds forming and reforming in front of their faces. Only a woman can appreciate the energy flowing between two men. But the thrust of these two together on the mountain of the signpost was so strong that Sheba felt herself being wrenched apart.

She forced herself to concentrate. Solomon's curly beard. His short, very slightly graying hair, polled in rows. Hiram's clean-shaven face, squarish. His long, full, amber ringlets. Why had Solomon waited so long before introducing them? And then she saw that the two men were utterly different from one another, hurtling apart at speeds like the planets'. Solomon had the gifts of administration and judgment. He knew how to accumulate wealth and mobilize other people's talents to his order. Sheba looked at him with the tenderness of a parent. In a corner of her heart she was his. And yet this Hiram his colleague, a man of no royal blood, was, it would seem, the chief cornerstone of all the great king's ambitious plans. He was true artist, true scientist. She realized all at once that she was in love with Hiram.

"My lord," she said to the architect, her eyes soft as cream and an otherworldly smile around the corners of her mouth, "what are the names of the three temples you have wrought on this height?"

Hiram, perhaps, had already fallen in love with her. She was a remarkable woman, she was the world. Between them there was perhaps already a bond: to do nothing that would offend the God of Love. And in conformity with this, their actions took shape around a core of perfect sexualness; all that was not erotic was burnt off and disappeared.

"King Solomon has names for them he will tell you," answered Hiram in a clear and smooth baritone. Solomon frowned, but was still. "I think of them," he continued, in the king's silence, "as the olive-wood house of spring, the midsummer cedar house, and the winter house of fir."

"Oh, yes, that's good!" exclaimed Sheba. Her eyes shone. "And Solomon will put his armory in the house of cedar, his wife in the house of fir, and the Torah stones inside the olive—?!"

"Well done," acknowledged the king. And to Hiram he said, "My Sheba is a treasure rare on earth."

Hiram's brows rose very slightly. He looked at the woman to see if she had become an item in Solomon's treasure house. He saw her quivering full lip under gaunt cheeks. So, bolder, he said, "Do you want to know more about the building of the Temple?"

Indeed, said the lady Sheba, she did. And so the three of them together spoke there on the mountain all the rest of the day, till the sun had wended its way around to the back of the house and the workmen had left the hill to take their sleep. They discussed the meanings of the various holy places, and the sizes and measurement ratios of the various chambers in the various houses, and the same of the many furnishings. Sheba often expressed surprise and admiration, and Solomon pretended familiarity but was himself surprised and impressed once or twice as well.

Until finally Hiram, with devastating nerve, took the queen's hand and kissed it, and suggested that they all three meet at sunrise the following morning to see the ascent of the celestial organ between the Standing Pair.

"Tell Sheba what the Standing Pair signify," said King Solomon.

Hiram paused. "They signify many things," he said at last. "Among which are the twin destructions: by fire and by flood."

Solomon had thought they represented good and evil.

145

"No, this is too lovely," protested the queen of Sheba. And she invited both men to her private chamber on this very eve. She was thinking of a lump of copper in a furnace, and an annealing by the hand of craft, and a goblet on a finely set table many times lifesize, and a drinking of her being, and the attainment thereto of all virtue. . . .

IN THE CHAMBER OF NARCOSIS

WHILE THE QUEEN OF SHEBA WAS TRAV-
ling to Jerusalem in state, with pomp and fanfare, making use
of seventy-five boats and six hundred load-bearing camels, her
first minister was going a different route. The brown-skin
priestess of opiates, a magicienne like her mistress, had ridden
hard over the wastelands on a flame-colored stallion with only a
small party in her entourage. In two saddlebags she brought
with her all the manifold intoxicant matters of a world
organized by dream and governed by hallucination: an orchestra
of narcotic and hypnotic, of delic and stupeficant.

This woman did not drink, but considered wine a latecoming
curse on the world. The cultivation of the substances in her
trust, and the lore of their handling, had been hers and her
predecessors' forever. In her first few minutes reunited with the
queen in Jerusalem she sized up the man-king, and determined
what it would take to dose him. Sheba's elaborate questions
and answers she thought harmless fun, but of no concern for
the final outcome of the encounter. While the queen spent
months penetrating the furthest recesses of Solomon's heart,
the first minister of Sheba busied herself with seducing as many
as possible of the men in Solomon's court.

That night in Sheba's chambers the priestess of opiates was
dreaming of the nyala deer exquisitely supping on the lace
tendrils of the mountaintop, invisible to the lion. She was
murmuring to herself, "May the noble one defy the manifold

147

creatures, Let phallus worshipers not disturb our sanctuary."

The men arrived with the queen. She woke and frowned. Sheba ushered Hiram and Solomon into the chamber of narcosis. There a silky red carpet, woven at the edges and at regular intervals with the colors of diamond, onyx, and sand, had been spread out to cover the floor, soft as low weeping. They walked on it with bare feet. The minister prepared some incense in a low dish and a pipe, which she handed to Sheba, and left. She ran her hand against the wall, ruffling the hangings.

Sheba looked at the two men, her lover and his friend. She touched her lips to the hollow white antler, and gave it to Solomon. And he to Hiram. And all together they drifted, as the smell of the mandrake berry drifted around them. Every flat surface became a door. The queen saw the Great One inside the space between every two dissolutions. King Solomon put his head back on a pillow.

"What was it you wanted to know?" asked the queen of Sheba dreamily.

Why was she taking the lead? Solomon hardly even wondered. His thoughts were coming widely spaced apart, like toll cities on the highway, with much desolate emptiness between. And by the time he'd gotten to a second, he'd forgotten the first, for it was so far behind.

Once long ago he'd asked the Old Man of Noah and Abraham and Moses and David for wisdom, and for understanding. That had been a moment like this one, on the mountainside at Gibeon, with all the polity assembled but he, Solomon, alone with the voice. Alone with the voice in a space more real than the twenty thousand souls around. Now he seemed to be alone again, lost on the modulations of Sheba's voice, and having a conversation (if his silence could be so called) this time with a God that was a woman in the prime of life.

The man-god had asked him what he wanted to have. Now the woman-god was asking him what, in his wisdom, he wanted to know.

In Solomon's eyes Sheba's outline was blurring. But instead of fading from his sight, as she had done during the riddling,

148

she was assuming every moment a new shape: all lovely, all based on her bodily form, but revealing aspects of her that he had never remotely guessed. He did not fear it; no, clinging to the wisdom that was his gift, he watched closely, and in a kind of hallucination he dreamed he saw her facing him naked, standing on the ghost of a lion, with the ghost of a lily in one hand and the ghost of two serpents in the other. Her hair fell down on her shoulders in two elaborate spiral locks he recognized as the Egyptian Hathor wig; then, in a moment, changed into a thousand Ethiopian plaits; and he saw her fine face black and gleaming, as one who had danced in the palace of the lotus queen.

And Solomon turned to Hiram, the architect, and saw in the three perfect bends of the man's body the grace that he, himself, would never have.

And the thought that remained longest in his mind was in no way human, but only a vision of empty winds whistling through the stones of a ruined Temple. Solomon put his face in his hands and people slowly came on the scene; he saw the barbarians who would over long aeons squat in the shadows of architecture now desecrated and abandoned, playing sheshbesh and chewing something that stained their teeth, and rising from their stupor only to an occasional moment of violence.

He would to groan, but the thought of his totally inadequate wife brought him back. Egypt was undead! There was still a sacredness intact in the king's chamber of the star temple at Giza, and perhaps elsewhere, a mystery of geometry and astronomy that—perhaps, yes—Hiram knew, and could tell him, if he would! Without premeditation, and in a voice the other two did not recognize, Solomon said, "I want to know when and by whom and how the pyramids were built." He seemed to want to add something, but lost the train of thought and broke off.

As Sheba considered this, a tender, heavy silence wafted over them like a cloud. Perhaps a winged thing was perched on the mother button of the Sheban tent: the free singer which brought Solomon and Sheba together, the bird the masons said split their big rocks for them. Or perhaps the bad germ was lurking about that can't stand to see a marriage, that same that was even now power-jealous of the completion of the Temple. Sheba noted with a sad sense of victory that Solomon's wife had added greatly to her understanding of this pyramid matter, while apparently withholding the information, for her own reasons, from her husband.

Hiram knew much, but he was considering that silence was probably prudent. He understood that he was in this room by the sufferance of the queen, and by destiny must always be a commoner in Sheba's and Solomon's royal play. And, even more poignantly, he knew that there were no rules, such as there would be among the brothers, governing this meeting. All this he thought clearly: the drug had hardly affected his strong metabolism.

Sheba closed her eyes and leaned back and spoke. Solomon listened. Hiram watched.

"The master artists of the Egyptian historical chronology you are inquiring into lived in an equilibrated, enchanted reality," she began. "In Egypt the goddess of the universe had twenty cities that lived under her elbows and kissed her knees when they beheld the universal eye upon the point. They lived as if under the influence of a dream. The center of life was the opium factory.

"Up from the desert came the wanderers, to taste the sacrament of the sacred opium called Thebe. The democrats. The communists. The families. Concepts were taught them by the Ogyges, the priestesses, the factory hands. The children demanded shiny brown metal circles. The grown ones quietly listened and imbibed. Many, many fell in with the way of life in Egypt and remained as celebrants of the immortal Isis, or of Re."

"You went there?"

"The Shebans visited the great pyramid and learned, and thence returned. They called us 'good students.'

"Of all these dreamers the most nearly awake was the noseless one's reedlike scribe Hesy-ra. I know him in my sleep though he lived long before me, and I will remember him always. From him I learned that records were carefully kept concerning the dreamwork. The road from the quarry in the mountains of freedom took ten of our years to build, and the housing itself on the site, twenty. That's all. But what we have kept of this old time is not the monument itself so much as the memories of the workmen. In the mountains outside Memphis the builders shared a high devotion to their common work, disguised from others. They understood the point at which art becomes science and both of these are subsumed into something even more human and glorious."

Now Sheba chanted in a low voice, raspy yet pleasant, like an older sister's:

"We build only for the mother, for the mother.

"We are every one of us thine.

"We will guard the beauty that is only thine."

Hiram was moved. Self-conscious, as one who never sings, he also began to chant under his breath, to the woman and the drowsy, transformed king, a song of the masons exiled:

"We create the land.

"In the to build

"And the to be built."

Then Hiram, speaking for the first time, sat forward and, a hand half-covering his mouth, continued the narration. He described how the brotherhood of builders pointed the tunnel from the depths of the earth to the earth's surface on a line with the polestar, the tail of the dragon, "the beacon in the sky," he said in a voice clean and low, "that the world turns around." He looked from Solomon's face to Sheba's, settling on Sheba's. Solomon was lifting his knees and prodding them, as if his legs were tingling.

"The one straight line," the king interjected, distracted.

"Yes," said Hiram the architect, now looking steadily into Sheba's eyes, and speaking without muffling his voice at all. "And this is all we really know. That the pyramids were here on the face of the earth poking up out of the ocean exactly and minutely northward, before there was ever sand in Egypt."

Solomon's senses were reeling. Sheba's presence had elicited disclosures from his master builder which all his own subtlety and gold had not been able to buy.

"U-h-who built the great pyramid?"

"King Cheops, they called Khufu," said Hiram.

"Philitia the shepherd, loitering about," said Sheba, "who never looked at it once."

And Sheba and Hiram took up the conversation among themselves, in voices still lower, fine and discreet, on matters that came fast and strange. They spoke of Chaemeranevti, goddess of the room, who built the third pyramid for her husband Mycerinus. They spoke of Hesy-ra's first graffito. They recalled to each other Chepera's ambition to sungodhood and his bird crown and his cat-woman totem.

"Immortal," said Solomon vaguely. "Are the pyramids immortal?"

"They are so far," said Sheba. Hiram laughed.

Sheba turned back to the king her host and told him what she believed to be the pyramids' original significance and function. That they were built to be communication towers. "My sisters say that an exchange like lightning took place between the clouds and the gold capstones on the top, and that long before the Horus worship we had—though we have lost the art now, as well as the capstones—a line of signal towers connecting the nations by way of the island of the bull all the way to the far north Cerridhwen land."

"Cerridhwen land, what is that?" said Solomon.

So Sheba explained that she meant the place of the blue men, blue, black, and orange, who wear the signs of their love and imagination tattooed on their bodies. "One follows such men with one's eyes," she began, but Solomon interrupted her.

"The Druids, you mean?" She nodded. "We routed them!" he shouted. "The cannibals! The wicked! The witching! The murderers of children! The devourers of babyflesh! The blood feasters! The bad parents! And, believe me, all the priests of that idolatrous crew!"

Sheba recoiled in her ribs, for she saw that Hiram was in agreement with Solomon's judgment of these people. "It was not a perfect society," she conceded. "But the Sidhe were warriors and poets like your father, Solomon, shameless and lustful, highly cultured. They taught us that the trees are older than the earth."

"The Tyrian sailors brought me back a Pict, once," said Solomon, suddenly milder.

"Of the totem of mermaid panther?" murmured Sheba.

"How did you know that?" said Solomon, a puzzled crease bifurcating his brow.

Sheba breathed one more taste of the leaf god and, slowly, said, "I know because I am, Solomon; but I think—there appears to be—there is a messenger demanding your attention."

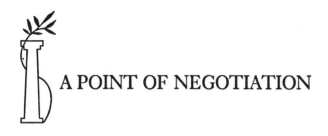

A POINT OF NEGOTIATION

THE MESSAGE CONCERNED AN OVERSEER of the Temple builders. Jeroboam was at home with a troublesome wound. He could not sleep. He could not work. He was delirious. He had a bad conscience. He was hearing voices in the sounds of chariot wheels on gum, of goats on the field, of dinner dishes. Foreign gods and judges were speaking to him as if to waylay him from the business of building the temple to Iao. Whichever way he turned he found new evidence, that no, we cannot do it.

Heavily, rumblingly, Solomon mobilized himself, hoisting his long body up from the red-carpeted floor of Sheba's chamber. Through the tent flap he walked, and out of the Sheban encampment, downhill, the air blowing in his face and reviving him, through the king's market and beyond, to the market of the prophets. Soon enough he came to the street in the Ophel district where Jeroboam lived with his wife and her family.

The woman greeted the king in an enclosed clay-brick courtyard, the smell of marjoram rising from a kitchen somewhere beyond.

Solomon passed a storeroom of food and entered a small chamber where his chief overseer lay in a sweat. He was scratching at some kind of bite on his neck. Solomon sat down on a low couch opposite and began to speak to the sick man.

"What's the matter, Jeroboam?"

"I can't go on working for you, Solomon."

His wife brought him in some lentil soup. He ate noisily. "Yes . . . ?" said the king.

As he ate, Jeroboam made his case that some of the building projects Solomon had assigned to the brotherhood were unjust. The repairing of the walls between the high places of Jerusalem and the newer residential districts, for instance. This internal barricade displeased the overseer, who considered himself a man of the people. Jeroboam, like Hiram, had been schooled in Egypt, where arm is raised next to arm in great beauty and strength.

Solomon was relieved to hear it. "A small thing," he said.

But no. Jeroboam went on to explain, sitting up now, his soup finished, how there was a lot of dissent among the builders. Solomon asked the overseer what he knew.

Not only over this question of the repair in the breaches of the Millo, said Jeroboam, but over many other things as well. "Like?"

"Well, wages."

"This will take some thought," said Solomon. And he settled in for some serious haggling.

Very late that night, after Solomon had gone down into town, the architect told Sheba the last few masonic secrets she had not known: he spoke to her chiefly of the destruction by flood in the time of Noah and Noema. How when the floods started coming the people of fire genius, the people who lived so much longer than we do today, built underground galleries in a desperate attempt to save themselves from the water. How they built tunnels down to the fires at the very center of the earth, where the ores arise all molten, and the jewels are as steam to be parceled out and cooled in underground veins, and the furnace pulse beats a hot, fast, intense life of man and woman. And how they intended to hide there, so brave and talented a people, leaving the great pyramid of Cheops standing immutable before the water, as the doorway and lid of all their tunnels.

This fascinated Sheba. She tucked her feet under her and

156

hugged her knees with her arms. "And when the flood was over?" said the queen.

Then Hiram told her of Tubal-cain, the one survivor of the great race that had fled into the hollow earth. The man who was descended from Cain. The man who was called the first technologist, for he built a tree of knowledge out of gold, silver, copper, and steel. This man, when there was only one other survivor of the underground race, wed her, his sister. And when the floods had finally gone, he and his sister and their son stepped back out through the small door he himself had closed upon the ancient world, through the pyramid.

And Hiram told Sheba how Tubal-cain and Noema found that the climate of the earth had changed. All around were rachitic animals and stunted plants. The sun was pale and cold compared to what it had been before. Below them, on the ground, were masses of sterile mud where reptiles crawled. In a sudden, glacial, infected wind, Tubal-cain took cold, and fled back into the pyramid, and died.

But his son by Noema lived on, though neither so tall nor so long-lived as his ancestors, and he took to wife two of the women who had escaped the flood in a boat. And all the genius of technology comes to us from this line, said Hiram.

Sheba was deeply affected. She sighed a long, deep sigh, a sigh of infinite longing, and the queen and the mason fell into each other's arms. And all that followed may exist only in the pages of an old but immaculately preserved book in the dust of the queen's chamber of the star temple, long and far outside the interests of manly history.

Now this Jeroboam in his prime was a striking man, with a weather-hardened face and flowing black and brown hair. The shoes he wore to work were the heaviest and the toughest that could be fashioned. Even in bed, he was a skillful negotiator. He had seen Solomon's fair guest moving among the construction workers and heard her questions in the arena. And he appealed to the king, "in the name of the Shebas," to grant him some requests on behalf of his men and himself.

Solomon's mind was on Sheba and Hiram. He let Jeroboam's

little trick go by—as if there were a plurality of Shebas, or queens of Sheba—and promised to bargain.

Jeroboam asked for more money.

It couldn't be done, said Solomon. Ten ingots of gold net to each of a hundred fifty thousand laborers and technicians, with bonuses to the more experienced and initiated, are all the foundries and food export would bear.

More money for the overseers!

"Jeroboam, do you call yourself a man of the people and then ask for more money for the masters?"

Stop the collection of tolls at the internal Jerusalem barricade.

Done.

"And get me your best doctor," said Jeroboam, speaking from the heart at last. "I can't stand this unease. Have him come to me and tell me and write down for me the names and methods of curing each illness as it befalls me or my men from the sky on downward to the head and the neck, and thence to malady of lung and loin and bowel, and even on to the decaying of the flesh."

This Solomon promised to do. So Jeroboam consented to come back to work.

And Solomon that very night wrote down his own and Joseph ben Barakhya's expert teachings on each of the sterile demon germs of time and every pair of the sexual genii, good and bad, of space. And this from Ornias the vampire flea who had put Jeroboam out of commission, through so many of the other monstrous demons of microbe and bacterium, unto Beelzeboul's son and grandson by the oak tree mistress of our electric world, who will destroy the universe in the end if we do not continue to fight him back: Amen! And the book in which Solomon's medical knowledge was written down was called the *Testament of Solomon.*

Solomon, growing a little older, felt a reluctant admiration for the purposefulness of Jeroboam. This man will be a king, he thought.

*   *   *

Hiram gently brushed hair out of Sheba's face.

The Egyptian slithered past outside their tent. A smile hit the middle point between her two eyebrows, and she began turning over the words she would use to apprise her husband the king of the circumstances.

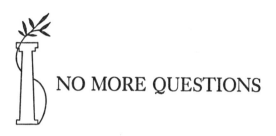

NO MORE QUESTIONS

THERE WAS A LITTLE RED ON SHEBA'S cheek, and some pale blue on the wings of her spirit.

Coming into the silken tent for a morning drink, her first minister noticed her smile.

"Did you lay with Hiram?" she asked, innocently.

"Yes, I lay with Hiram," said the queen of Sheba. "And the night passed quickly, and at the light I was awake and refreshed, though I had not slept. And I remember the rounded line of his arm that came across my breast, and his large straight hand in my hand, and the almond smell of his long hair, and his face that is uncompromising and beautiful."

"How was it?" asked the minister.

"He said, 'I have always loved you.' And I said, 'My friend!' And my body was several-flavored and sweet for him. And when I felt his blood moving in his pale, smooth chest, I heard that my own blood was moving in the same way, in the same time, and I felt that we were being tuned together."

"Did you take by him?" asked the minister.

The queen of Sheba looked back at her, her face as blank as a white moon. "You are a priestess and first minister of the land," she said, "but I am queen over you forever. Ask me no more questions."

The minister disappointed, impudent, partially candid, tiptoed out of the tent. I shall narcotize and sleep with Solomon, she thought.

*   *   *

When Solomon was told what had transpired in Sheba's tent after he had left, a paroxysm of jealousy and rage passed over him. His wife remained lurking in the doorway to his apartments. She was ready with a suggestion; she was all support.

Merely to acquiesce to her will in a small thing, she ventured, for hadn't she been a good wife (A good wife! As if the Egyptian had even come close to the Sheban in wifing me!) and didn't she always want to help him in everything (And precisely there, she was most useless!). Then the woman suggested that Moloch the seven-leveled one would soothe his pain. Solomon went red with disgust. But for the moment he had no fixed point of reference. His wife wore a tiny silver hand on a chain around her neck.

And merely at the price of the smallest possible sacrifice. Five flies, say. Or five locusts. A pittance.

Solomon in a fit swatted five flies. Nodded angrily to the woman. And hastened out of his room and out of the palace, heading toward the Sheban encampment. The hill glittered with stones. A dry sirocco blew over the city from the direction of the plains of Jordan, where Hiram had cast that basin so large the people were calling it "Solomon's Sea," in which the tumult and tempest of the waters of creation were recalled. A wind blew against Solomon's dark face and soothed it a little, bringing a memory of his father, but he was plagued with the new thought that he shouldn't have given in to the Egyptian woman's wheedling, and her unknown purposes, for even a moment.

Sunset purpled the sky and made the stones pale. Outside the Sheban camp a gust rattled the thistles. A flock of sparrows suddenly flew up from some low bushes, startled at his approach. In the past the birds and he had always been in tune. He tried to drive the sad thought out of his mind.

Sheba came to him quickly, and they walked together through the Temple grounds, past the basin of bronze with its water for two thousand baths. They descended into the Kidron, toward the vale of Gehenna. He was walking fast. She asked him to stop at a round fortress constructed of the debris David had left when he broke through. A pure wind blew up the

162

leaves of the olive on the hill across the way and showed their silver undersides. Sheba held her breath; she saw in the way Solomon was narrowing his eyes that something awful was about to happen.

Finally he began. "Have you entered into the place of infinity with Hiram?" he asked.

"Yes."

"Will you go there again?"

"Infinity is probably inexhaustible, Solomon."

Solomon picked up a stone and threw it, with an arm that was not weak. They watched it fly, and saw the light glint on it for a second, and heard its dull landing in the brush. There were tears in the corners of his eyes.

"I cannot share your wisdom, lady," he said. "I think you must choose."

Sheba saw Solomon's eyes had become large and black like an orphan's. But in a very distant corner of her heart there was a bird still singing, constant, high, and wild.

"This is fraudulent," she said softly. "In choosing I have already chosen you, for he does not require it."

Silence. And the wind. And wasn't David struck by the angel of Death one time when he interrupted his work on the day given over to study, to go listen to the wind sighing in the trees?

So Solomon threw himself into the business of the Temple. For several days he avoided the queen of Sheba, and spent his time instead with Jeroboam and the other overseers. He moved among the journeymen and questioned them randomly. He ordered that the status of the miners be elevated. As the work neared completion, the king found he was of two minds about it. For one, he wanted to astonish posterity with the perfection of his construction. But he had also tasted the sourness of betrayal, and no longer took pleasure in the genius of his architect.

He decided to consult with the old priest Abiathar, an eerie soul, who had been the only survivor of a massacre in his youth. Abiathar was not his friend; he had favored Solomon's brother for the throne, and Solomon had long ago stripped him of his priestly office and sent him into suburban exile.

So the old man was surprised to see him when the king arrived unannounced at the priest's estate outside of Jerusalem. "Then the Temple is almost finished? I'm glad to hear it. You know I don't get into town much anymore," he said dryly. "But why come to me? You have a high priest who serves you better than I."

Indeed, Solomon had a high priest in Jerusalem, but he had more confidence in this lonely old exile. Abiathar was perhaps the last ever to know the secret of divination by the stones. "Son of Eli," he said, "you know I come just because you have opposed me in the past. I admire you. I need some unprejudiced advice."

Abiathar nodded, and bade Solomon sit; and the king told the opposition high priest all about the building of the Temple, and the Temple architect of contoured person, and the queen who came down from the south to wreak havoc in his house. Shock, disbelief, horror, and wariness passed over the old priest's face by turns until, when Solomon had finished, all these were replaced by his long-unused professional expression of pious compassion.

"Have you committed this to the brush?" he asked first of the king who sat trembling.

"Not the whole thing," answered Solomon. "The earlier part has been recorded by my secretary in *The Book of the Acts of Solomon*. But of the latter, nothing—"

"Good," said the priest definitively. "Leave that to me." With his left hand, he began idly to shape the working part of his brush in a point. "You know I bear you no animosity, Solomon," he said, "least of all for the long exile you have imposed on me. All this time and solitude have brought me to a very gratifying labor. The nature of which is perhaps not unknown to you—?"

Solomon mumbled an ambiguous assent. The fact was that nearly everyone connected with his illustrious court was engaged in some sort of ambitious endeavor, and the king had no idea what had been occupying Abiathar all this while. But it was with little surprise that he learned now that the old priest

164

was writing a long history of the world: from the creation of universal man in the finitude of the temporal and sensible sphere, up to the present.

"I understand from my colleagues who graciously visit me here at Anathoth that this work will be influential," the priest said. "And for your sake I tell you I shall edit the account you have given me of these events, in order that the chapters concerning your administration take on their most instructive form. And thus it shall be, a small thing."

Though Abiathar's solace was as intangible as a word painted out, Solomon felt enormous relief. He recalled how difficult it had been for his father to get certain things taken off the record.

"But as for you, my King," continued Abiathar, "the Temple is your genius. You must see to its consecration with all your gifts, and no distraction. Take a rest in the south," he suggested.

"Well, that's easily done," said Solomon. "The king of the rock" (by which he meant Tyre) "has asked me to join him in Aqaba as soon as possible, in order for us to send off the gold fleet."

"Very good," said the priest. "Go to Aqaba. Don't think of anything forbidden. Remember the spirit in which your project was conceived. Prepare the speech you will make when the public worship shall begin. And, above all, son of David: give of your learning and your love and your very substance to the Lord."

Solomon made a gesture so quick as to be almost invisible, as if to kiss the hem of the priest's sleeve; then he shook his hand heartily, thanking him. And hurriedly remounted the royal mare for his return to the city.

MASONIC WAR

BACK IN JERUSALEM, SOLOMON ORDERED his things be packed for the trip south, then he thought to make one last circuit of the Temple grounds. He put on a white wool robe, and walked past the many workmen in the courtyard outside the Temple walls. Further inside all was, by order, quiet and empty. Solomon stepped alone through the twin columns and onto the portico where it was cooler. Fragmented thoughts occurred to him with regard to the speech for the people. Building built I (he thought). The high house to you. Place for you to sit. Forevers. He loosened the neckpiece of his heavy robe.

Slowly, dutifully, he entered the hall of shimmering gold that was the main sanctuary, filled with the dizzying goldworks. His eyes glazed. He crossed to the holy of holies, guarded by its supernatural beasts. He pushed aside the curtain and stepped in.

So this is what it's all about, thought Solomon. Here in the darkness of the small cubicular room were the Moses Stones in their box—dank, irregular, stolid—the inheritance of a slave people confused and weary from a hellish escape out of the grandest civilization on earth. And here was where he and Sheba had lain. Now he leaned against a wall of the chamber, and thought, For this bed is too short that two neighbors may rule therein together.

Solomon stumbled out of the Temple again, his eyes

blinking from the gold and the sunlight, and as he did so he nearly collided with an unlikely knot of men engaged in argument. By their tools he could see that they practiced different trades. Drawing a discreet distance away, the king heard their breathless exclamations:

"He has enslaved the carpenters to the miners!"

"He has subordinated the masons to the miners!"

"He wants to rule over the miners!"

"He gives his strength to strangers!"

"He has no country!"

"The journeymen are brothers!"

"The ranks have equal rights!"

"The work is ours!"

The threat in their sentiments was clear, but not their precise argument. Still shaken by his visit to the adytum, Solomon shrank from a confrontation. Instead, he memorized the appearances of the three men, and went to look for Jeroboam. He found the overseer in the shade of the brazen sea.

"Why did I see a miner, a carpenter, and a mason standing idly together just now?" asked the king. "And why would such a confederacy feel a terrible, racking hatred for the work and for their master?"

Jeroboam smiled up at the king with cat's eyes. "Oh, that could describe a lot of people," he said.

Solomon squatted beside him. The sun beat down hot. As he sweated he recalled that the priest had told him to avoid distractions. "Tell me about them," he said.

Jeroboam was almost laughing. "Tell King Solomon? Why should I? Oh, I guess you've cooperated with me. I'll tell you now; but listen carefully, because later I may be too busy to talk."

"These are poor men," said the overseer, wiping his brow and tensing his jaw. "Honest and ambitious. They would like the title of overseer, or master. But they lack talent—or luck—or whatever you call it. They have pressed Hiram on this score, for rank and salary. But he has had to refuse them. So their hearts have gone to ruin in greed and envy."

"Who might they be?"

"You want names? Well, it might have been Phanor the Syrian mason you heard just now, and Amrou the Phoenician carpenter, and the old Jew of the Rubenite tribe they call Methousael, who is a miner." "What are you telling me, Jeroboam? There are no Jewish miners." "Well, then, it could have been Sterkin, Oterfut, and Hoben. Or Sterkin's cousin Starke. I understand Abiram is a very dangerous fellow. So is the one known as Kurmavil, or Romvel. And some Egyptians by the names of Haemdath, Haghebomoth, and Hakhibouth." "Egyptians?" said Solomon. "Akiroh, Gravelot, and Gibs are a problem." "So many?" "These are just the ones I know."

Solomon considered this. "This indistinct wrath. Is it directed toward the king?"

Jeroboam weighed his words, juggling caring and uncaring. "Not really," he said. "Your power is secure for now. I would say these ones see no further than the grand master of mixed race who pays them their wages."

"You mean they are the enemies of . . ."

"Hiram."

Solomon rose. As the overseer stared complacently after him, he walked away from the brazen sea in the direction of the palace. He had not yet embarked upon his rest cure, but his brain was already on holiday. A plan was forming itself in the ooze beyond consciousness. Crossing through the broad Temple court, King Solomon stopped and said a few words to the three nobodies he had heard before.

Then he made all haste to Aqaba.

The two lovers whispered together in the candlelight of the Sheban's tent. Their clothes lay awry, mixed with the silken hangings, in corners beneath slender ebony poles. As they spoke Sheba recalled as if it were the simultaneous present all the places their bodies had been in the hours just past, and she drew from this memory-dream a forbidden, humorous warmth. Hiram's hand now rested upon the inside of her arm.

"When you swung the hammer to make the bronze cistern ring, you were the very god of the planet for beauty," she said softly.

A smile crossed slowly over the architect's face, filling his lover with joy. The queen smiled back at him, a smile on the verge of laughter, and rested her hand upon his hand on her arm.

"And your wisdom is as profound as Solomon's," she continued, "and more practical."

Then Hiram rose to better see his love, leaning on his elbow, and ran his hand gently, with a geometer's care, and with force equal to her resonance, along the subtle place where her side abutted upon unyielding rib. Sheba, this is Sheba, he thought.

"What sublime luck!" he whispered, "to be alive when you are alive!"

Now the woman reached out and buried her hands in her lover's curls, her eyes playful and radiant. "You mean, you think I'm good-looking?" she laughed, despite herself.

Hiram grabbed the queen of Sheba and pulled her to his chest, and hugged her with the speaking need of his arms. "You are the sun at the equator," he murmured. "You burn me. You make me want to close my eyes."

And then their flesh lost its sensation of separateness . . . and they began again to play the game each had known for a thousand years. For Sheba it was as if Hiram were the first man she had ever believed in. His reality permeated her. His life flooded her limbs. In all parts of him she knew who he was and approved.

They stayed like that a long time, in the tent pitched on the farther hill, listening to the sounds of the night outside the spiritual city. The big animals, free of their trainers, spoke to each other in unearthly tones and pitches. In the palace complex there was still bustle and light, though all around, in the hilly tiers, the city people slept in darkness. An occasional goat nagged to be let out of its stable and into its master's rooms. At two or three spots along the wall, lute players and harpists diverted little clusters of the adventurous, the insomniac.

To feel themselves closer, Hiram and Sheba pretended that everything outside was an enemy. They clung to each other. And the theme upon which their love played its endless variations was an old one of doomed, priceless sweetness.

170

Behind the closed eyes of the queen and the architect there was bliss in blue and green and violet and mauve.

Then Sheba wondered what had passed between her and King Solomon. The penetration of enigma? A judging?

"You loved him," murmured Hiram, reading her mind. And there was no spite or jealousy in his voice, just a sad grandeur.

"You could be king by a movement of your eyelashes," said Sheba.

Hiram laughed a little, pleased but not credulous, and took her hand and pressed it to his heart. Suddenly Sheba said, "We can't stay here forever."

Hiram let go of her hand and looked into the shadows around her eyes. "I have no fatherland," he said, "and no parents but the spirits of the air that taught me my craft. I will wander the earth with you gladly, sweet Sheba, my sister, my wife, my angel of light."

With their souls in their faces they kissed each other again, and agreed (for it occurred to them both at once) that to journey out of Solomon's kingdom together would surely provoke him. So a lovers' plan was made, and the Temple architect resolved to leave Jerusalem alone at the first opportunity, traveling north toward Tyre, only to come round to the queen of Sheba again at last by a long and indirect route.

And thus. On the last day. So many magnificent constructions of the mountaintop were finished—the queen's palace and the king's palace, armory and treasury, the villas of the palace people—but the house of habitation of the invisible Lord was yet hours away from completion. The grand master was in the nub of the Temple cleaning up. As he worked he dreamt and planned, on the verge of a journey northway to his adopted home of Tyrus: thence to assume the purple mantle of Lord Hiram, called Adoniram, and travel due east by the double rivers; and finally, with luck, and some few companions, to turn south, the very antipodes of his flight from Solomon and from the Jerusalem he would see no more, to meet his love in sweet reunion on her own distant, fertile land. It remained only for him to pay the workmen.

They had been gathering all day, from all corners of Solomon's empire, lining up to receive their wages. One hundred fifty thousand men filled the valleys from the capital as far as Jericho, winding over the land like a human serpent. Below their feet hung the great lime quarry. In their hands and pockets were still the tools of the day: hammers, scissors, axes, mallets, chisels, mauls, wedges, levers, knives, compasses. The fresh air evaporated the sweat of work. They spoke to one another, and took easy poses, and relaxed. Each one rehearsed to himself the sacramental word he would utter one last time into the paymaster's ear. They could smell the gold.

Jeroboam's eyes were lit with excitement. He slapped his fellows on the back and repeated till he made himself hoarse, "It's only the beginning! It's only the beginning!"

As they waited the men discussed what they had built. To some, the structures were too big, to others too small. Carpenters who'd erected the high walls saw them loom, and praised the Temple's height. Metalworkers admired the bronzy pillars along the Temple sides, and how they supported the wider upper storeys, and praised the spreading. A story went around that before the queen of Sheba arrived Solomon hadn't been able to get the big arc of the covenant through the door; but when she came, it fit right in. There was laughter. The king had gone away to inspect some boats, and everyone felt free to make jokes at his expense. The end of a work of many years was a happy occasion, and stimulating. The men's clothes were dusty, their beards overgrown.

Of course, among them, too, were some whose manner was constrained, whose eyes moved restlessly.

Having completed the last clearing away of the dust of the tools, Hiram stood before three huge drums of gold ingots facing his hundred fifty thousand men, and motioned for them to begin to approach. One by one they stepped forward, through the Temple lobby, and pronounced a word to the paymaster very low, according to the hierarchy of their functions, and were individually paid by him. Hiram listened carefully, his senses calm and alert. And he realized that even now, when reward was so close, and ecstasy so nearly possible for all, there were apprentices and companions from among the

172

masons, here a few, there more, pronouncing the disruption of their trust, a very call to arms. This the architect considered in the storm eye of detachment, alone with his logic, and then he heard it again: "Shibboleth." He tried to ignore it, to pay fairly, as he guessed appropriate, as he remembered a man's rank. But somewhere far distant, beyond the Temple doors, far down in the valley of Gehenna, the grievance lived, and the battle song was ringing.

Shibboleth basade korea baruach
The river current on the land sends forth its web
    of meaning, according to the holy spirit,

Meomes garinim ki rav
Under the burden of the stones which are its master,

Uvermerchav harim yom kvar yafuach
And from the chariot of the mountains the day is
    already a prediction

Hashemesh ketem vezahav.
The day cuts short in gold.

To Hiram's shock, one man standing before him anticipated receiving his payment, and rudely grabbed for it. This would not have happened in Egypt, reflected the engineer. But this was not Egypt. Suddenly the orderly line gave way at a weak point, and the troops in a great surge burst into the Temple. A resounding thud of feet rose up, as flesh in all the tints and shades of the Levant covered the black and white tiles of the Temple floor. There was shouting.

Three men in an extremity of tension and anger confronted the grand master, demanding money, satisfaction, the truth.

Hiram stood his ground. And found himself, curiously, thinking of his student days. Assassins with raised arms and awful faces were approaching him. Calm air over the Nile. Perhaps I should have studied harder. A hammer. Power had corresponded to wisdom, there, and the requirement for entrance into the sanctum was constancy and virtue. A chisel . . .

"It's struck!" somebody cried. And Hiram staggered and went down slowly, slowly, like nobility. He was thinking about eating cucumbers, and imagining the shadow of a triangle against the horizon, godly silhouette over ocher sand. This Temple was nothing, he thought, as his weight hit the floor, and settled, resting over the space of three large tiles. Compared to the temples of Egypt. This Temple . . . he thought . . . could have been a banker's house in Memphis. . . .

He was bleeding from the head and side. "There's a point of the compass in his heart!" someone shouted in alarm.

And then there was nothing but chaos and riot. Loyal masons fell upon the attackers of Hiram but, in the crush of bodies eager to liberate the wealth around them, the guilty escaped. Eruptions of fighting continued for hours. Finally at twilight there fell a stillness, and the corpses of able men draped around the money coffers seemed to be merely asleep. A carpenter lit a cheroot, and shared the light with a hewer of wood.

Hiram had been left for dead in a rubble of gold. But he was alive. When the shouting subsided, he rose from a corner of his great work and left the temple precincts, still bleeding. He knew the blood would never stop. Behind him all his life was flowing away in a stream of crimson glory. He pressed toward the tents. Toward the scent of Sheba.

And he found her, she found him, she loved, they loved, with love as intense as death, passion as incomprehensible as the grave.

As she drew her tent flap for the last time, the queen commissioned an errand. King Solomon was out of town, and not likely yet to have heard about the events on the steps. But his domain was small, and the news would reach him soon. Sheba therefore dispatched her first minister on a fast horse to head off all the other messengers and distract him for a while. The woman would take with her some qat, some cannabis, perhaps a drop of cherry-pit poison.

The first minister of Sheba galloped half the length of Solomon's little kingdom, all her muscles standing out hard and taut as whipcord. Finally, at about the time the other messengers were just setting out from Jerusalem, she found him and the king of Tyre in their camp at the southern port. The town of Aqaba had the uniform and monotonous aspect of an enclave that had been built all in one burst, and to a single purpose. The air above the slaves' row houses hung thick with smoke from the copper foundries.

Solomon was gracious and unsuspecting. He brought the minister of Sheba out to the harbor to look at the armada of refinery ships in the soft darkness. She stood with him and his ally there at gulfside, fatigued and staring blankly at the murmuring lip of the sea. Nor did the two kings say much. Soon Hiram excused himself, and Solomon and the first minister of Sheba retired to his pavilion. They exchanged words. And then, with a guilty smile, he took her into his arms.

Deep into that night, when dawn was only a guess in the east, the sky split open in a furious lightning storm. While King Solomon lay drugged in his shipbuilding town on the Gulf, the first minister slipped back out of the royal pavilion and onto her waiting mount. Sheba had mobilized her thousands. The body of the queen of Sheba's last love lay buried in a grassy knoll outside Jerusalem, underneath an Egyptian gum acacia with mud around its roots.

And the great Sheban caravan was decamped. Beneath a black and pink sky furrowed with violent white lights, as winds unloosed thick and heavy rains over the hills, the Shebans had turned and gone back to their homes. Only the scribe ben Barakhya saw it, standing upon the palace roof in the storm. The Arab watched as the long line of men and animals from the land of women gradually disappeared into an uncertain horizon.

A messenger arrived at Aqaba.

"Then very good," said Hiram king of Tyre, when he heard. "The sacrifice has been made. The Temple in Jerusalem will stand."

175

"No!" cried Solomon, leaping to his feet. "What have they done? I didn't tell them to kill him!"

Over the gallop of her camel the queen of Sheba turned to her first minister and shouted. "Did I go virgin to Jerusalem only to return from there pregnant?"

"I know what you mean!" the first minister shouted back, and dug her heels into the flame-colored stallion, and rode away.

 A BOOK

Aɴᴅ ᴛʜᴇꜱᴇ ᴡᴏʀᴅꜱ ᴡᴇʀᴇ ʀᴇᴄᴏʀᴅᴇᴅ ʙʏ ᴀ person of letters close to the events: the urbane Hiram of Tyre, perhaps, or perhaps Abiathar, high priest in exile at the time of Solomon, who lived to see all three kings of the united monarchy, and the massacre of the priests at Nob, and was present on the battlefield the day the Ten Words of Moses passed into the hands of the Philistines.

"And the queen of Sheba," wrote Hiram or Abiathar or someone else, "heard what was to be heard about Solomon of the unspeakable IAO, and came to try him with riddles. And she came to Jerusalem with a very heavy army, camels bearing spices, a very lot of gold, and a rare stone. And she came to Solomon and spoke with him of all that was in her heart. And Solomon told her something of all she spoke, that there was no speech hidden of the king which he would not tell her. And the queen of Sheba saw all the wisdom of Solomon, and the house that he had built. And what he ate; and how his workers were organized; and how his officers were positioned; and what they all wore; and how his crops were grown; and his most valuable property, when he ascended to the house of IAO. And there came to her no more anger.

"And she said to the king, 'True was the speech that I heard in my land on your speaking and on your wisdom. And I had no faith in this speech until I came and saw with my eyes. And here is what was not told me: half again of wisdom and good to

177

the hearing which I heard. Men of the goddess, workers of the goddess, these standing before you always hear your wisdom. Thus does IAO your judge (blessed be his desire for you) give you, on the throne of Israel in love of IAO, both Israel and the hidden world. And it will be the king's pleasure to do judgment and righteousness.' And she gave to the king a hundred twenty weight of gold and very many spices and a rare stone. At no other time did spices like that come, which the queen of Sheba gave often to King Solomon.

"And I also, Hiram, who carried gold from Ophir, brought in from Ophir sandalwood trees: very much sandalwood, and a rare stone. And the king made of the sandalwood trees pillars for the house of IAO and for the house of the king, and violins and lyres for the men singers. At no time did such good sandalwood trees come, and they were not seen until this day.

"And King Solomon gave the queen of Sheba all her desire, whatever she asked for—not counting the catastrophe given her by King Solomon. And so she turned, one hundred eighty degrees, and went to her land, she and her workers."

BOOK THE FIFTH
AN OLD MAN'S MADNESS

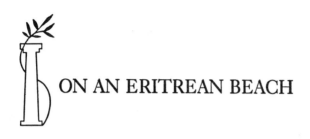

ON AN ERITREAN BEACH

SHEBA FLED SOUTH, HER BODY SEEKING the cleaner rain and rivers and the relaxation of planetary centrifugal force toward the equator. She sailed with her retinue through the Gulf of Aqaba, avoiding the powerful Nile civilization to the west. The floating queendom skirted the desert bank where, not far over the dunes, lay the oases of Mecca, Medina, and Jidda. En route, two hearts beat in her body.

In the Hamazen shore region of Eritrean Ethiopia, the queen of Arabia and Africa stopped and made herself a childbirth bed on a slabby rock. Night winds of a warm winter solstice soughed along the beach, through the sparse vegetation. The queen felt a longing for rites, or structures, or (perhaps most of all) Solomon's and Hiram's sleek chiaroscuro Temple. But there was nothing of man's work for her here, now, in the stark lowland.

To the southwest, men were carrying treasure of stuffs back to their homes. Army and beasts had gone on ahead. Only a small entourage remained. Men in pearl-encrusted belts, with red gold on their wrists; women flirting, watching, or attending the queen and the sacred fire.

Sheba lay in a cleft of a big gneiss, ruminating on what she had done. It had been imperative to lie with the genii of Jerusalem. She saw no blame, no fault; the trembling weakness undermining her system she attributed to the pangs of birth.

181

But now she was feeling another imperative. To erect some kind of monument to the genii. In her arteries was flowing the mother rule that had flourished in the southern parts of antiquity—but in her veins was flowing the father rule, that was coming inexorably down from the north to supplant it.

The queen's women were plying her with narcissi, Solomon's "roses of Sharon," carried over the water in ice chests, that the birth be auspicious. They hastened in their languor. There was not one among them who did not sense the portent. Once she had borne a child, the queen could no longer be called virgin. She would have to go into coregency with her heir. But there were many problems with this succession. The child had been conceived on foreign soil. And if it were—heaven forfend!—a male, then some other, perhaps a daughter of the first minister, or the princess Little Brother, would inherit. All remained to be seen. The queen groaned and turned to a side, resting all her weight on one slender elbow. She moved as if inside her the infant were a great cat, restlessly stalking its escape. An attendant straightened the veil over her. None spoke or gave directions or comfort, for the virgin in parturition was deadly.

Awkwardly, the queen sat up, and took a small chew of qat. The pains were insistent now, but the herb took them a distance away. Suddenly the queen imagined she heard a bit of a ruckus at the edge of the sprawling camp. She could see the blue and white costumes of three young men of Judaea being denied entrance, and she motioned them through, as if taking a simple break from business.

When they reached her, she said to them, "What do you want?" in Hebrew. The nearest retainers would be shocked. Hebrew! She must have given too much of herself to those people.

Two of the boys knelt down and kissed the toes of her sandaled feet, while the tallest, a skinny thing just come into manhood, made some kind of Levitical greeting or blessing. Then a torrent of poetry burst from their lips, coloring their young cheeks. They told her that the king sought her, that he loved her, that her beauty surpassed that of the daughters of Jerusalem. Then they told her, in their own words, that

Solomon had never been so distraught. That his Egyptian wife had become a different person, and entirely impossible. That he was indeed begging her, Sheba, to come back to him.

Sheba listened with a faint smile. She had worshiped at the fountain of the king's words. Sometimes his brilliance had touched the very root of her. But other times she had suspected that his fine-wrought phrases were unacknowledged quotations from the other brilliant poets and philosophers in his court, and she mistrusted him for it. Hiram's death had made her understand, for the first time, what Solomon had meant by that devil he believed in, who instigated evil, and she had lost the will to trust in Solomon's ambiguities. She had come to know the limits of his ethics. And even though this was what she had set out at the first to discover, she had never realized to what extent she herself would be drawn into the experiment and hurt by it. And so she remained cool to the impassioned plea.

She replied to the young men royally and formally, using the words from their song. "I am a cavewoman and a noble-woman," she said. "My beloved is the first man on earth and he is radiant."

Around her the Shebans were directing their energies toward hallowing this birth and sanctifying the anticipated daughter. Forgetting them, Sheba drew a gold ring from her arm, an emblem of her office, though the Judaeans did not know it, and tossed it to Solomon's young Levite. The heel of her hand slipped and struck the ground for an instant.

"Fetch some water!" she cried, abruptly.

And late that night, the baby was born. His name in the northern language was Other-Self or Son of the Wise Man; though to the last there were some in the woman tribes who called him I Chose My People. By the laws of the south only a daughter could rule in Sheba. But the queen (though she never cared to speak with anyone, neither her first minister nor the librarian, nor any other, about the boy's father) seemed to have no further desire to know man, nor to produce any other heir.

For she had decided—in the long hours when her insides were tearing to release this soul, during the searing and the pushing between the moments of sublime relaxation, when at the last his skull was crashing and crashing against her bone—

she had understood that it was this child, and this love, that must be raised up. Whatever laws needed to be changed to commemorate her time in Jerusalem in the person of this being, Queen Sheba resolved to change. Even, she thought, her consciousness dissolved in the tranquillity of quat, if it meant that a male was to interrupt the line of queens who had ruled in Sheba since time out of mind.

A THOUSAND WOMEN

FOR FORTY DAYS AFTER THE DEPARTURE of Sheba, from the barley harvest through the counting of the weeks to the wheat harvest, Solomon ate nothing but barley bread and grew gaunt.

He could still fly in his mind. But his flights were no longer the unitarian ecstasies among the conference of the birds such as he had known in his youth. Now he flew by the eagle power of his mature and achieved majesty, in cloud and storm, to the mountain behind which a male and a female were forever chained together.

After the war among the masons, the survivors were traumatized and numb. They agreed to bar women from membership along with fools, atheists, libertines, the too young, and the too old—by which it was hoped to avoid such bloodshed as they had seen. In the fog of self-recrimination, the only person who seemed to have kept his head and was now using the situation to advantage was Jeroboam. The overseer rose quickly in the brotherhood. He began to call with insistency for a workers' revolution. Solomon realized that even his mother's favorite prophet was supporting Jeroboam, and sent killers after his former hireling. Jeroboam took refuge in Egypt. And continued to organize the Israelites from there. He criticized Jerusalem's dividing wall and denied the importance of the Temple work. He attacked Solomon's taxes and his labor policies. He let it be known that if he were king the arrogant

Levites would be replaced in the priesthood by men of the people. His campaign slogan was: "I will awake Miriam's tambourine for you, and we shall dance again around the Golden Calf!" Throughout the populous northern tribes there were a great many dissatisfied, especially masons and women, and very few who claimed a close blood relationship with the reigning monarch, and so they rallied to Jeroboam. With a well-armed Libyan bodyguard, the former overseer appeared to have the greater part of Solomon's kingdom within his reach.

In the rich metal lands of Edom to the south, prince Hadad had returned to lead his people to national independence. The bereaved population remembered the genocide in David's generation and still chafed in slavery under Solomon. This Hadad was a formidable enemy, for he claimed to be a half brother to the king, and yet played both ends of the Davidic house against the middle. He held up the family's hidden ignominies, like a basket of reptiles, for all to see, that his own position might be thought superior. Up and down Edom they spoke of the rape of Tamar, of Absalom's incest, of the suicide of Ahitophel. Hadad was a breath away from the throne.

The northeast was also threatening. Around the sophisticated trading center of Damascus, Rezon's gang had parlayed a profitable business in red wine and fine white sheep wool into a military stronghold of the Aramaean tribes. They were biding their time; history lay on their side.

And in mighty Egypt where Solomon had looked for alliance, armies were massing under the most ferocious general that land had ever known. And he had his eye on the Temple, and its gold.

But Solomon did not think about politics. For it is written, after Sheba left, that King Solomon took wives upon wives, where before he had had only one. In the years that followed Solomon took a thousand women, from as many bloodlines as he had had workmen, so many different women as he could find in Canaan and all the surrounding lands. He took women-chiefs, and queens, and princesses, and lawful mates, and unlawful mates: concubines, and slave girls, and the captured.

The little princess from Tyre was one of the first. She came to Solomon's bed humbled, because she had been in Jerusalem while Sheba was there, and she knew how happy they had been. Still he found some consolation in her, because of the gold her father's men knew how to fetch, barter, and steal. The men of Tyre and Sidon and Byblos, their salaries paid by Solomon, sailed through the Gate of Weeping to the outlying districts of Sheba called Ophir—and returned with great wondrous lumps of the red gold, and the green gold, and the yellow gold, that the queen had given Solomon in tribute. The gold of Sheba will build Jerusalem, thought Solomon, in pain.

His Moabite wife came from a line that worshiped the god Peor with nudity. A woman of great experience, the Moabitess lay with Solomon while elevating one of her feet in the air, setting upon that foot a burning oil lamp, without in any way impeding the relation.

He took Edomite women, soft and red-skinned. And he took hard, bony wives from among the Hittites, who rode horses and worshiped the storm god Taru. Crafty Jebusite women from Jerusalem came to him on business or matters of judgment; and these he wed too.

And his men brought back prisoners from the distant tribes: so beautiful, so unconquerably hating and proud, that even to look at them made the skin crackle. Mulattoes, carried to the court of a rapacious potentate, they had come to know flight, and theft, and aggression; pain smelted their flesh to the bone and made it simple.

In all these women Solomon saw ghosts of Sheba. Distractedly, he studied them. He indulged himself in long speculations upon the roundings and joints of their thighs, and upon their statures and features, and upon their smells. He addressed them all as "djinniyeh," female genie, in wishful adoration. The women blurred into a parade, a new lap every fortnight, and each one the king set up in a little house of her own. And in this way Solomon denied that his empire was crumbling.

Threatened on every side, Solomon's cosmopolitan court and capital were as oblivious as he, and spent their time in bedroom talk. David had had many wives, but Solomon's style was different, flamboyant, upsetting. It was rumored that when the

187

queen of Sheba left, Solomon had cursed her one time, and that (he being a man of powerful tongue) this curse had been uncannily effective, that it had taken on the tangible form of The Cursed One, King of the Demons, and that this entity had moved into and was inhabiting King Solomon's body. It was said further that The Cursed One was engaging in sexual perversions in the name and person of Solomon (not Solomon himself!)

"What kind of perversions?" the Assyrian chariot knight wanted to know.

Scholars and scribes whispered among themselves. They were conditioned not to speak in direct language about such things. They reported officially only: sleeping with his socks on, crying for his mother, taking the women in their courses.

The knight was disappointed. He knew some better ones.

A Kurdish horseman invented the parable of the horses. "Solomon," (he said), "in his enthusiasm to inspect a thousand steeds, has missed the time for prayer. He will slay them all in repentance!" (said the Kurd).

A nomad tribesman said: "Solomon boasts that he will have seventy warrior sons by seventy different women. But he forgets to add the divine conditional. He will have no sons!"

A sheikh, who had stopped in Jerusalem to buy a fancy utensil for his home in the wilds, disagreed with these two, and declared Solomon immortal in the garden of perfume.

One of Solomon's in-laws, uncle of the king's eldest children, daughters Little Spice and Little Penance, bruited it about that the queen of Sheba had been a strangler of babies. His friends made bawdy jokes at her expense. If she were the first woman on earth, alone with the first man, they said, she would dispute with him the manner of their intercourse! The Ammanites called her a goat, an ass, and a goose.

"But no," said a Chaldee with fat cheeks. "The queen had the royal spirit of a bird."

"She was a lioness," smirked the Assyrian: "the best fornicator in the jungle."

"At least," said a Levite, "Solomon's getting a lot of home cooking."

The women said the Egyptian deserved it. If she hadn't

gotten vicious during the Sheba affair and after, Solomon would have stayed with her.

A Gibeonite soothsayer told the Chaldee about a new spell on the subject. It was "Shabba(s) Shalom." The people were being told it meant "Good Sabbath." But the soothsayer avowed its real meaning to be "Sheba and Solomon." A Greek leaning on a spear nearby nodded agreement: "Ao Sabao Solomono," he said, adding a reference to the deity to make it all perfectly kosher.

The Egyptian herself, tormented and bitter, prematurely old, handled her difficult new situation as best she could. After raging at Solomon and weeping herself to sleep had proved both useless and disfiguring, she had her artisans carve a delicate model in alabaster of a maiden swimming toward a gazelle. This meant hieratically, "I aspire to wed the king"; and it suggested to her that no matter how many king's wives there be, no one but she could ever hold the place of King's Great Wife. While this was not much, it was all she had. The alabaster gazelle swimmer was made into a pipe, and she smoked from it.

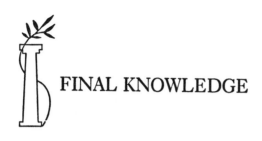

FINAL KNOWLEDGE

IN THE BEDS OF THE DAUGHTERS OF ALL the nations, Solomon's mind expanded to exploding. Relentlessly he rooted out the gods and secrets in all their strange hearts and made them his own. Moloch the chief of awful sacrifice. Melkarth the strongman. Milcom, God-King. He came to know Demeter the barley goddess, and the heavenly Ishtar under so many names. Now when he saw cows he worshiped Io, and heather recalled to him Isis. The priests said to marry was to know. And Solomon knew too much. He had heard the thousand voices of the invisible, and the theocrats called him idolator.

Until at last the corridors and passageways of society dissolved for him, and the king whose name is wisdom found himself once again in the primordial cave, this time alone.

There he made his final search. Jedidiah, Friend of Ja, the son of David, came at last to the place of his heart's desire: the pyramids embedded in gold, dusty with the residue of ages, without a door. His soul (strangely unencumbered by his body) sought an entrance. The feeble, almost-dead souls of three ancient departed kings helped him. And he went down the wormhole of time. . . .

Inside the tomb of the millions of princes, millions of horses, millions of corpses, guarded for centuries, he passed beyond artifice, descended suddenly in surprise, battled weaponry with theology, heard the living voice of a forgotten language; and in a palace to which the keys were gold, silver, brass, and iron, where pearls could never become eggs nor gems be crushed for flour—Solomon came face to face with the void where aspirations end, and he conceived of the magnitude of vanity.

Mirage, he said, and vapor. Air of emptiness. The hallucination of hallucinations. Breath of emptiness. Vanity of vanities; all is vanity.

And he lost the ring which Sheba gave him. Solomon came back from the tomb tattered and emaciated, his mind burnished by the winds of another dimension, no longer interested in writing, but only a preacher, dry-as-ash. The people hastened him back to his throne, saying, "Come, return to what you were." But the king only laughed oddly, in a way that unsettled them, and brushed off servants and wives.

"There is no memory of first things, nor of last things," he said. "Nor shall there be memory among the later people. . . . Words bleat. And yet the eye is not satiate with seeing, nor the ear filled with hearing."

His subjects were perplexed and angry that their profligate king had come to this. He no longer seemed to want to govern or to judge. He was irritated by his throne, uneasy in his palace. He wandered the streets of his own capital among the lowly, and traveled the seacoasts looking into the bellies of fish.

"The king is mad," said the old general Benaiah.

Seventy elders sat in a semicircle of benches in a court partly within and partly without the Temple. They looked at their president dubiously. "What is your evidence?" "How do you define 'madness'?" "All our kings have been mad."

The retired army commander spoke over their ancient cracking voices. He had developed a flabby neck and jowl in the space where his governmental cranium had lost touch with his soldier's body. "At the mountain of Gibeon, where the king asked for wisdom," he said, "he slew a thousand oxen." He paused. "But at the departure of the foreign queen he slew not an thousand, but an thirty thousand!"

Actually what was worse, to Benaiah, was that for months now Solomon had snubbed him. He who was first in the king's service, who had been his best friend. But he didn't feel he could use this as an argument before the great court.

"It is for the Levites to decide a matter of ritual," said one elder wearily. A murmuring went up. A rustling of robes. "The Kohen has anointed him." "Solomon's reputation is as good as the Temple," said another. The late afternoon sun slanted down in the western plain, putting half the courtyard into shade.

"Ask him if he wants some fresh grapes—and if he says 'yes' then we'll know he's mad—because they're out of season!" "Be quiet," someone rebuked the last speaker.

"The priests have abandoned Solomon," said Benaiah then, with a statesman's rhetorical grief. "The prophets speak of secession. The national security is at stake—we must cure him!"

"There is no cure for madness," came back an old, resigned voice quickly.

A hush fell. Between the sun of day and the coming out of the suns of night the discussion of the long-aged scholars hung lost beyond time. Was the king mad? And what if he were? What had been divinely revealed on the subject?

At length one of the old men stood up and walked with great deliberation to the front of the assembly, where he found a spot that seemed right, with his back to the pillared side of the holy house. Long ago this man had been the best student of the best teacher. Now a silver beard hung down his chest. And he stood so still that the smallest motion of his arm or head seemed significant to the others. "We intervene at our peril," he said, very, very softly. Benaiah closed his eyes in resignation and listened.

"All the rustic nations have kings who make war and plague the peace with their greed and folly" (he went on, just a little louder). "Who but we, who have separated ourselves, would choose a king to whom the secrets of the world are revealed? Is it for us then also to judge him? Shall we treat him like a bumpkin in a delirium, with broiled lean meat and dilute wine? Shall we provide him with a duplicate ring to replace the one he has lost or thrown away?

"And if our king has become a prophet?

"It is not for us to comprehend that which is without end, but only to preserve. Let us return to the planting of the soil, for soon we shall eat the first of the olives from the trees that were put in the earth after the Temple was dedicated. And let us care each for his own household, for that is the most precious thing we know. And as for the national security" (here he turned to Benaiah), "it's always best for the courts to be lenient in the really difficult cases."

Once in his wandering Solomon made for the country of Amman, where his parents' nemesis Uriah the Hittite had met his death. Distraught, amnesiac, atoning, the king of Judah and Israel applied to the Ammanite king for a job in his kitchen, and indeed worked there for a cook for a time. Then the spell passed; the motives dissipated and were forgotten. When Solomon came to his senses, such as they were, he was again king in Jerusalem, with the princess of Amman for a wife, and a son by her called Rehoboam, Great Nation, his first legitimate male-child.

Now as Solomon sat in the hall of judgment that had once been a game room, dandling Rehoboam on his knee, his thoughts turned to Sheba. He recalled the afternoon she said that something he loved would be divided. His nearsighted eyes closed, and in the phantasmagoria of insight he imagined that the child the women had been fighting over that day was his own kingdom: young, fragile, vulnerable, that he had inherited from his father—and that this kingdom would be divided, as he had suggested the child be divided so long ago, between tiny Rehoboam and the mason Jeroboam. Their names fused in his consciousness, as he tried to fuse the kingdom again: Roboam. He fell deeper into dream, and heard the icy clear voices of the Great Green Sea, and of the Great River; and they said, in their different tones, that they would soon reclaim all the wealth and treasures that he, Solomon, had collected of them. Then the king began to shudder, and his legs and feet to shake, until he had to call for a servant to come and take the child back to its mother's apartments. Was even the kingdom real, then? Had he squandered everything? Was all not a mirage? Of itself, he felt his mind turning again to Sheba.

In the end what was spoken of most was the missing ring. Though it was such a tiny thing, and beneath the attention of the Sanhedrin, for Jew and Canaanite alike it came to seem the very essence of the mystery of the king's transformation. Everyone had a theory about where it had gone and why. Some blamed its loss on the princess of Sidon because she worshiped the graven image of her father. Others blamed Djera'de, the concubine, who'd given birth to illegitimate sons. Some said that Amina, the Hidden Female, had possessed the emblem of power while the king purified himself, and had been induced to give it away. Others declared it stolen by Sakhr, the spirit of trade.

Storytellers along the wall at night said the ring had been aligned with the forces of the sun and the moon and the five heavenly planets, and chiseled at the first by Irad, genius of the ores. A few remembered that Sheba had called it an inheritance from her Himyarite ancestors. Here and there a mason spoke of Enoch the builder and space traveler, who had owned it awhile.

One suggestion about where the ring might have got to was made in a mud-floor hut over a clay stove by a plump Jerusalem housewife. Pouring some milk into a stranger's brass bowl, a hand on her apron, she allowed as how Solomon's Temple-building demon must have it. For whatever restless spirit had showed him how to do all those things on Mount Zion in the first place, she said, wiping her red face with her arm, and inspired him to keep all those men away from their wives for so long—and didn't we see so many of them lovely men lying at the foot of the altars and all around the holy rooms at the end after all, their lives just dripping away, and they in great pains—such a one must have taken Solomon's very heart and soul.

And wouldn't taking his ring be easier?

A CHILD'S EDUCATION

A MILLION BELLS FILLED IN THE SPACES of the harmony rainbow. Someone played the long flute. A woman was nodding her head from side to side. Feathers fluttered from her ears. Many people stood in their places, who did not dance, their heads also moving, filled with the potion of the music. It was a dance of winter and sadness, known to every spine. Far away in summer the music would change, but how that might be done was known only to the saints. The woman in white lifted the water bowl slowly to her mouth and drank. A cow sauntered through. Kettledrum and bird whistle called forth the further, distant spirits.

The eyes of Sheba loosed their grasp. Talk was so much chatter. Only the music spoke, and now it spoke of war. A warrior's bitter necessity to fight. Determination. Sticking to it. A question was raised by the tambourine and sistrum and answered by the bass. Two drummers seemed to be struggling for control. The flautist felt himself alone and sang a celebration of conquest. Then soloist became magician: angry, wise, vengeful, canny, a terror. Notes flew from his ax like blood.

The people's breath hung on the music, begging for release: "Give us a dance!" At last the musicians, like gods, complied.

The years passed in Sheba, and Other-Self grew up nicely shaped and full of vigor, monarch to be of all the big sprawling land from Fetch Some Water across to the Ramlat Sab'atayn;

and westward to Shaba where the Congo rises; and far to the southern aZeeb. He played with his age mates and understood without troubling about it that his mother was the first citizen in all this great space, and over all these cities and mountains and rivers bearing her name. And when the time came, he went to school.

Now the child of the queen of Sheba was given an education different from that of all the generations before him. For though she had fled Jerusalem, his mother had incorporated into her thinking much of what was believed there. He would not spend his childhood dreaming in the gardens or strolling about the grainfields by the harem. He would not stay close to his mother and her sisters and learn at their knees. Rather he and his childhood friends would be dispatched to all corners of the empire, to study with tutors, and learn from each their special knowledge.

The first thing he was to learn was power. It would be good for him (she decided) to hear a broader tale of that pivotal Asian-Achaean war than she herself had heard. Not to dwell so much on Penthesilea, Amazon queen, and the Ethiopian Memnon, her ally. Rather Menelik (as his tutors called him) would be exposed to sympathetic descriptions of the men of the winning side: Achaeans, Aeolians, Dorians, Ionians. He would learn the names of the heroes who defeated the Amazons in the various cities.

And studying war, he would analyze the struggles on the Sheban continent too: between Ethiop and Egypt, between chiefs Umbopa and Umhlopegazi. He would string his harp with arrows.

To this end Menelik and his companions climbed long ropes to the cliff colleges outside addi-Saba-ba, where women missing breasts and frail, jocular, defensive old men recited litanies of these past events, and instructed the youth in the use of weapons. Below in the grassy plains they were taught to manage the royal parade beasts: horse and elephant.

Then buxom nurses sat with them in round huts near the mountain passes where once the snakes had been and lectured reluctantly on animals and crops. And everyone was relieved when, at the end of a lesson, they were free to ramble on together about health, happiness, and the sky.

The Sheban boys and girls hunted birds in the Nilotic marshes of the north, to improve their concentration. In the lake boats Egyptian technicians, balanced one-footed, spoke tersely of jewelwork, textiles, and music.

They were brought with solemnity into the library in the oval palace and shown the letters and the books, and the librarian's priestesses seduced them into long afternoons of intercourse with hieroglyph and calligraph.

In winter they went south for panther, and in the evenings after hunting they gathered under the bronze-green castor palm, as slim, confident Yemenites and small-nosed Africans discoursed with them on love, marriage, and the baby times. It was then they sang the songs the Egyptians had taught them, and the old Sheban love poetry, and the war chants, and the philosophical couplets of Arabia. And they practiced the curious up-and-down dances.

Sheba still ruled in Axum. But she was mellower, less irrepressible, took fewer risks. The parade bed throne had been dismantled and she held court from an austere rock pavilion no other woman was allowed to approach. It was there she liked to think. In memory of Jerusalem, and the Temple mount, she had had constructed two gigantic pillars in gold-encrusted granite.

There by the pillars, and especially when the sun rose exactly and minutely between them, Sheba thought of Solomon, and of the man they had both loved. How simple it would have all been to a Sheban, she thought, and how hard it was for Solomon. We might have been comrades together even now, imagined the queen of Sheba, in the splendor of a double empire, no, a triple empire, that would have adorned the world! Even as we spoke that last evening in the valley near the spring of Gehenna, I thought that we were still speaking as intellectuals, in the riddling mode, I thought there was still a chance you might see things as I did. But war struck my camp suddenly and unmercifully. I fled. And that, I suppose, means that you won the contest between us. Are you happy with your prize?

I hate you, Solomon.

But I shall always appreciate your genius. Your culture creates all of our histories. Our civilization is vastly superior but unarmed. My people cannot afford to be ignorant of yours. The civilization of the fathers, the eclipse of women into domiciled brides, overtakes the world—as evil (so late I understand!) so effortlessly overtakes innocence. Your form of evil is bound up with power . . . and my people shall know it, God help them!

Men over women! It is a flinty knife! Yet the change is coming, and let us make it for ourselves in the best way we can. I shall send back to the land of Solomon and Hiram for wise men, hoping they bring here with them the wit and science of their masters—but no, such things lose color in an emissary's head. More likely we'll have to make do with emblems and implements. Trifling things, like the phylactery, circumcision, the sabbath.

When he was twelve years old, the son of the queen came to her to ask who was the author of his days. Soon now, any moon, he would join the circle of dancers, and he knew already the movements of their graceful bodies. But a companion at ganna hockey had said something troubling on the subject of fathers.

Sheba took the mirror she was holding and held it to Other-Self's own face. He looked at the metal, smooth and reflecting as a pool, and saw, first, a kind of yellowish haze all round the back and outside of his head. Then he saw his own shining night-colored hair, with leather strips and cowrie shells in its long waves. And then he noticed his own wide, dark, dreamy eyes. He looked away, feeling it would be improper to see any more.

"You are he," said Sheba.

"Who was he?" said Other-Self.

Sheba saw he was not to be so easily satisfied. But in the time of his telling she felt her own old age. "Before I met your father," she said, "I knew many men according to the ways and laws of Sheba, men in whom I took my joy, men who did not know me, men whom I afterward discarded. I did not destroy them—as the barbarians and the snake queens do—however; I felt myself above that. But they had no throne, no rights over me, no privileges. And if they had tried to boast of me or sell the secrets of my bed however casually to any other soul, indeed, if they had even breathed the suspicion to a friend that

I was not a virgin, then they would have been slain as liars.

"But your father," said the queen of Sheba, "was a man preeminent above ten thousand." And she stopped, to think of him.

"How was my father different?" said the boy, with something earnest pushing into his eyes. The queen his mother reached out with a ringed hand and touched the shells in his hair. A tear formed. Hurriedly she took him into her arms and hugged him. And when the moment was past, she told him about his father's body. That his father's head was a crown. That his hair hung down in rings, noble as an Arab's. That his eyes paused Greek and fecund beside the thought-stream, washed with milk. That his face was a formal grove, his speech like all the musky herbs. That his hands were wands of gold, full of minerals. That his prick was a magnificent engine, wrought ivory, wrapped in the writings. That his legs were finely shaped as marble. That the aspect of him (she said to Other-Self) was like snow on the mountains, like cedar, excellent; and his palate too was sweet.

"I don't know anybody like that," said the boy.

So the queen of Sheba at last told him that his father was not a Sheban, did not live in Sheba, had not known her in Sheba but in a distant country. And the boy understood the enormity of it. His face changed. And she saw that he had understood. For by the laws of marriage with a stranger, a most powerfully binding custom, the queen had communed with a foreign man on his own soil. And this meant, irrevocably, that her inheritance must pass to that man's line and to his people.

"I have cut you off from your mothers," said Sheba, with stoic cheeks. A thick band of worked jewels shone from her hair, and more jewels swung from her ribs and hips over a thin dress, dyed pale red with safflower. "You cannot inherit the fading light of Sheba. But I shall see you inherit the way of the men."

And when the boy had bludgeoned his first rhino to death and come into the full measure of youth, even with the earring of maturity, Sheba, as her last official act, declared that there should no longer be any woman on the throne of Sheba but only a man, and that henceforth the rites of paternity should be established. Tamrin thought the debarment fascinating. Little Brother, who thought she had a right to be queen, was stunned, shocked, and impotently furious. The first minister took it the hardest: she overdosed herself; Sheba buried her after the style of the Judaeans. Then the queen of Sheba had the late librarian's three high priestesses engrave upon pewter that the children of Sheba worshiped nothing whatever in sky or earth beside the To Be without Non-being. And she took a new man into her bed and was happy.

So a new kind of consciousness came blowing down from the hills and mountains and volcanoes of the north that shouted the old soft jungle truths to an astonished silence. The serpent of Mount Bor was fed a poisoned goat and died once and for all, and with it, the echoing commands of goddesses and mothers. Myriad erosions and perversions of the queens' old authority rushed over the land like a river seeking a new course where all is flat. The life-span of man, that had been growing shorter since his creation, crystallized at seventy years, for the blissful innocence of love no longer sustained him. And it was Sheba, the last matriarch of the old civilization, inheritor of the earth from the dinosaurs and the fallen moon, who had been sought by the king of China and who had herself gone to see the king in Jerusalem, who chose this.

SOLOMON RAVES

I WHO SPEAK TO YOU WAS KING OVER Israel in Jerusalem. Now I am old and certified mad by the priests and scribes and law professors and I lean on this carob cane, walking my dusty feet through these huddled streets, touching the walls of houses on both sides, knocking at your door, begging with this strangely carven bowl for some milk, some honey. No? Will you give me barley, then? All right, sweet householder, barley for the preacher, who was the wisest of all men, and is now a demon in eyes, my white wool robe dirty, my soft laughter disturbing to you.

Do I regret that I tithed your grain then, and took away your husband as I pleased for the palace work, and made you send me all the fine animals? Ha. None had a throne like Solomon, nor plans more worthy the attention of the fifteen-hundred-year-old eagle. By the genius of my father David who stole iron from the Philistines and water from the Jebusites was I born, in the sun of the beauty of Bathsheba my mother, in the cool air of friendship with the great King Hiram of Tyre who—ah, but is that your daughter? Come to me, little one.

How can I regret? Seven hundred women have I known by the document, and three hundred outside of it. Whisper to me in the court of cedar that there dwelt a beauty in a court ten chariot months distant and she would have been mine within the space of eighteen chariot months. What a man I was! (Thank you, little one.) And yet all but one, no—

203

The barley is sweet and reminds me of a wedding. Excuse an old man's melancholy.

There was a woman, once, came to me from the south, that had a lion's beauty and a mind like diamond, and to her I lost my wits. I did not know it at the time, and you must never speak of it. The architect of the great judge's Temple, himself, fell before my rage. It is proof of my madness. The priests and scribes care nothing that I killed my brother and my cousin for power. But when they consider that I killed my friend, an artist, for love . . .

I was no child. My brain had already spoken to me of love, and in my youth I had conceived the plan to rule the world. The daughter of the pharaoh of Egypt would be my wife, and when she came to me, she would bring the secret of the Egyptian civilization. I demanded as dowry the architects of the great pyramids. The whole earth trembled. Seers whispered that together we exceeded our bounds, that a countervailing power would arise in the northwest. Our bridal bed had a canopy pierced with all the stars of the heavens in their places. And to the wedding feast she brought a thousand musicians each with a different instrument and a different god. About that I was still so brash. I thought I could collect such things with impunity.

My mother was worried. The priests of the oracle were worried. We stayed underneath that canopy looking at the star jewels dancing overhead for a long time that first night—or maybe we didn't come out for a week; I don't remember. At any rate the redoubtable Bathsheba entered the bedchamber, at last, on a pretext.

The princess of Egypt had taught me the stars, and much else. But Sheba undid me.

Sheba appeared to us just as the Temple was being finished—I am forgetting exactly how she came, or what brought her, or if I knew of her first or she me—but I know that I felt it had all been built, with all the wealth of the earth, for her. The great hunger that I had had for power, and for fame, and even for wisdom, melted away, and I was satisfied in her, and all I wanted was to converse (and dally, you will say, but you will not be entirely right) with her forever.

Jedidiah and Maqda: that was a love! Ten thousand souls were we for each other, with a new face each two seconds, by the genii and djinniyeh and—damn them!—demons of my holy court. The nosy and ambitious scribes followed us around, and lurked in the corners, that they might catch our words in their brushes and black gum and iron it down onto the parchments for their own forevers. That the shards of their libraries be shattered! Nothing can be remembered of the past and all is repetition. Only the pale recollection, like a scent, of certain moments with her and how I remember I felt about them then, hangs in the span of my life like a tiny flame of heaven: warming, feeding, giving credence to . . .

But don't tell the scribes that. Because when they saw her leave they forgot how they had loved her too and remembered only what could be most easily passed on in idle chatter over a penurious lunch. They never knew The Great One Who Takes Captive in all her magnificence. They saw Sheba only as a courtesan at the end, and in their receding vision she became queen of the demons. And I, The Friend, The Peaceful, became for them also The Accursed.

The princess of Egypt was livid. She worked on my pride, calling me "cuckold." I weakened. I sought reassurance. I buried my head in a thousand women's mysteries only to find them stale, flat, of this world. None could speak or think or feel as Sheba. After the behavior with the women had exhausted the patience of even the most loyal followers of my father's house, children in the muddy streets began to joke about my cock feet; "the king wears socks in the harem."

Mortification grew. I dealt as I could with the charades of kingship. I put down for a while the heroic Hadad of Edom, who had a sacred grudge. I battled back Jeroboam, also, whom my father-in-law harbored against me. Some one of them will bring down Israel at the last. I can feel it. I shudder for the magic he will gain. I have dispersed my amulets, I have concealed my ring in the depths of the ocean.

And yet I imagine that there is a David II, a son of our proud lines, illegitimate—like Solomon himself in the sight of men!— but for all that heir to this mighty kingdom, and to the blessings received by Noah, and by Abraham. Would he be wise, and worthy of instruction? Could he subdue the ill fever that took my builders—and protect the Temple in Jerusalem, and the Sheban library besides, from the whirlwind, and the trouble without a head, and the trouble with too many names, that seek to undo them?

If David II should come I would make for him a parade of interpreters with golden headdresses and plumaged birds on their shoulders, and behind the interpreters I would send out harpers and minstrels, archers and boatmen and chess players, and men who know the ice of the north. Whether he be wise or silly he should learn everything that I have learned from women, all that I have gained in talking with my queens.

I can see his fine nose, his black hair! Let him come to me— and then I shall forget Hiram the architect at last. And then at last I shall lose this awful fear and dread that my Temple must fall.

Ah, can you please, just a little milk for the end of the barley? You, little olive skin, so seductive with your averted eyes, your stance in the doorway with torn linen shift hanging over your skinny hip. And you are tantalizing me as Bathsheba did my father, some say when she was only eight years old. There is no justice. There is no wisdom that does not alternate with folly. There is only vanity. Come closer, pomegranate lip, give me just a little milk—!

Such Facts as Are Known
About Solomon and Sheba
in the Various Cultures

It appears Solomon was a historical figure. Archaeologists have found traces of multiple horse and chariot stables, copper foundries, and a shipbuilding city, which they date to his period, almost exactly three thousand years ago, in the middle of the tenth century B.C.

It is not altogether clear about the others, however. Some scholars still dispute the existence of the legendary queen of Sheba, as did the rabbis of the Talmud, and Voltaire, before them.

The difficulty in establishing the queen's authenticity derives in part from the antipathy of the current residents of territories identified with ancient Sheba to the intrusions of archaeologists. This is especially true of Yemen, where archaeologists think they have the best bet for Sheba (or Sabaea) in the remains of a giant dam in the middle of the desert. There are also related buildings, including one popularly called Haram Bilqis, or "sanctuary of the prostitute." Moslems believe that Allah caused this dam to break and waste these lands because they were pagan. Consequently there is, on the one hand, a superstitious dread of the whole area. On the other hand, the Arabs would like to recycle the old stones for use in modern buildings; and they tend to get a little overbearing, like threatening rape and murder, in their concern that foreign diggers not find something like a solid gold statue of the queen.

While most archaeologists now agree that these ruins in Arabia Felix probably belong to the civilization of the queen of Sheba, there are other ruins and other claims all along the eastern coast of Africa which are still a riddle.

In Zimbabwe—the name means "stone buildings"—there is a long-standing popular tradition connecting a massive elliptical palace and a fortress acropolis with both the Ophir of Solomon's gold mines and the residence of the queen of Sheba. It is in this setting that the absolute ruler called the Monomatapa lived, as recently as 1830. However racial politics have so far obscured the study of the place, and no relics at the site have been dated to earlier than the time of Christ.

Ethiopia has the most elaborate claim on the ancient name of Sheba, but it is based more on the national literature, both folk and epic, than upon the obelisks and temple around the old holy city of Axum.

For a long time Western scholars disputed the Ethiopian versus the Arabian claim, tending to favor the latter. However, recent scholarship points to linguistic and racial affinities between the two areas, and postulates an ancient business connection and alternating political conquests. Because the one is by convention "Africa" and the other "Arabia," they are almost never shown on the same map. Yet the fact is that Ethiopia and Yemen come to within fifteen miles of one another across the Red Sea at Bab el Mandeb.

There is abundant evidence, from Herodotus, Strabo, and Pliny, to the present, that a person very like the queen of Sheba is a distinct historical possibility. Ethiopia is known to have been a mighty empire at the time of the Trojan War. Though her power declined from that point, in the early Christian era Ethiopia was still considered by historians to be the third-ranking power in the world. Similarly, historians have called ancient Sabaea in Yemen "the richest country in the world" in its time. Scholars concede that a queen in this area is plausible. Hitti, the best-known historian of the Arab world, says that worship of goddesses preceded the worship of gods, that mother right was formerly the basis of economics and kinship, and that polyandry—one woman, many men—was practiced. It is archaeologically established that there was correspondence, in the time period in question, between Assyrian kings and Arabian queens.

For the history of Solomon and his court, the hardest documentary evidence is the Bible. I have used this as my *New York Times*. But it is by no means the only source. In three thousand years the mythology of Solomon and Sheba has spiraled out in time and space from their original meeting-point in Jerusalem, taking on new expression in at least a dozen other ethnic centers and cultural traditions. The Bible story may occupy a special place in our heart, but it has long ago become deeply implicated in layers of legend from many other reliable sources.

In the libraries of the West there is more to be read about Solomon than about Sheba. Solomon's nation still boasts integrity, the monotheism he personally flouted still cherishes him as a hero, his invisible Temple is still the magnet of a tradition. By contrast, Sheba is misty, imaginary, nonlinear. He is situated. But the remains of her life and breath and flesh have been scattered all birds' flight out of Israel to Persia, China, India, Arabia, Yemen, Egypt, Ethiopia, Axum, Zimbabwe, and the Congo. In general, the farther one goes from Jerusalem, in any direction but that of Europe, the more the queen of Sheba appears as the heroine and protagonist of the dyadic tale.

The meeting of Solomon and Sheba is described briefly, simply, and classically, in the Old Testament, which may have been set down before 600 B.C. The two appear again in the New Testament, even more briefly. They are rediscovered in a fresh light about A.D. 600, in the Koran.

Within the next few centuries Babylonian-Jewish, Byzantine and Coptic Christian, and Persian Islamic commentators were the first to add important elaborations to the story, without contradicting the basic Scripture. Where the Bible had said only that the queen asked Solomon hard questions to test his wisdom—the writers of the early Christian era indicated what they thought these questions were. Where the Gospels had called her only "queen of the south," and the Koran had described her as a sun worshiper—these writers filled in extensive details about the queen of Sheba's origins. And to the Biblical account of Solomon's royal power, and the Koranic account of his magical power, the writers of the early commentaries added an account of reversals in King Solomon's later years.

The son of Solomon and Sheba arrived on the world literary scene in the thirteenth century, when an epic of his birth and maturity was written in (or translated from the Arabic into) Ghèze, the classical language of Ethiopia. Based on preexisting oral traditions, as it is said, the Ethiopian national epic Glory of Kings was used to bolster the legitimacy of a current emperor. And the tradition of Sabao-Solomonic emperors in Ethiopia is still alive today. In 1955 the national constitution identified Haile Selassie, né Ras Tafari, as a descendant of these two personages. Selassie was deposed by revolutionaries in 1974, after a forty-four-year reign; but his followers in the Western Hemisphere, the Rastafarians, enliven the Caribbean with their Old Testament prophetic fundamentalism, their reggae music, and their trade in "herb."

Simultaneous with the appearance of the dynastic Solomon and Sheba in Ethiopia, there came to light in Turkey a Sufi, or mystical Islamic, Solomon and Sheba, whose love was considered base.

The Crusaders imported from the Levant a formal and ceremonial Solomon and Sheba, whose image was painted in or engraved upon cathedrals in Italy, France, and England.

Around the time of the European Enlightenment, a movement called speculative freemasonry originated in London, laying claim to continuity with the builders of Solomon's Temple. The masonic tradition offered a new interpretation of the relationship between Hiram the architect and

Solomon and Sheba, and elaborated on the circumstances (only indirectly alluded to in Jewish tradition) of his death.

My biggest surprise in doing this research was discovering that the Talmudic rabbis didn't believe in the queen of Sheba at all. The Talmud is considered to be the written-down "oral law" of Judaism. And the Talmud says that the woman Sheba is a mistake in translation, that the Bible word translated "queen" should rather be "kingdom."

Others are as upset about this as I. The remark has been called anti-Ethiopian. It has been noted that the author of the remark, circa A.D. 250, was himself a putative descendant of Solomon, and anxious to defend his family against the dishonor associated with the queen.

But why dishonor? As my research progressed, I came to see that the Jews have always had a hard time dealing with this woman. When they are not denying her existence, as here, they are maligning her. In the Middle Ages the cabalists called her a witch and queen of the demons. Recent fiction by Jews in America has described Sheba as either too pushy or too homely for Solomon to be attracted to her. (It's true the Arabs have also been known to call Sheba the daughter of demons, but a parallel legend dismisses this one as lying slander. And the Arabic tradition has generally treated the connection between the two monarchs with sensuous respect.)

In the Jewish collective unconscious, Solomon is the best kid in the class, and a macho hero to boot. As a brief and mysterious pagan interlude, Sheba loses all her selfhood to him. She becomes a void, an other.

To right this imbalance I resurrected an unfamiliar tradition about Solomon from another part of the Talmud: that toward the end of his life the king was mad, that is to say, possessed by the king of the demons. And it was my feeling that it was his encounter with the queen of Sheba that drove him mad. Though the imagery of king and queen of the demons is horrendous, expressing archetypal disgust and disapproval, it does have a certain symmetry.

Because the Rosetta stone was deciphered by comparing proper names (Cleopatra and Ptolemy mainly) in its three scripts, I resolved not to invent any proper names in this story.

Maqda (Magda, Makeda, Macqueda, Makera, Makere) is the name of the queen of Sheba in the Ethiopian tradition, along with its masonic and Egyptian variations. The Greek-Latin root suggests "greatness," and recalls the Arabian *mahdi,* "leader, guide." All the rest that the minister says about the etymology of the name comes from a good English dictionary, a Sanskrit dictionary, and a Sanskrit grammar. I drew upon Sanskrit not only here, but also in the queen's and the first minister's dreams, and in the pythoness's trance, because of a Theosophical premise that the queen of Sheba was an adept in the wisdom of India.

The name Tharbis for Moses's first wife, an Ethiopian princess, is given by Josephus, a Greek-Jewish historian from the time of Christ.

Two distinct characters named Hiram are mentioned in the Bible in connection with the Temple. One is "Hiram king of Tyre," with whom Solomon conducts economic diplomacy. The other is "Hiram of Tyre," whose plebeian lineage is given, who comes to work personally on the Temple in Jerusalem, and whom King Hiram refers to as "Hiram, my master." Various Biblical passages say that the latter Hiram of Tyre either superintended the work in brass (which would have been extensive, since this was the Bronze Age), or all the work. The masonic tradition takes the latter view, and greatly exalts the role of the master workman, whom they call Hiram Abiff (a phonetic rendering of the Hebrew for "my master") and other names. There is some lingering uncertainty about the expression "Hiram." Some scholars believe it is a dynastic title rather than a proper name. Later Jewish legends say that King Hiram lived a long life but suffered a horrible death and was doomed to hell for thinking himself a god, while Hiram the master workman entered paradise incarnate.

Nor have I invented any major characters. Solomon and Sheba; David, Bathsheba and Nathan; the nameless pharaoh's daughter; the two Hirams; Benaiah/Son of Ia, Jeroboam, Abiathar, and the prophet of Shiloh, are all Biblical, and I have respected their Biblical biographies. Solomon's difficult relationship with his mother is not stated, but is I think implied, in the Bible. The lustiness of David—his escapades, the personalities of his wives, is a big theme in the Talmud.

It seems to be true that the Talmud favors David over Solomon. The Koran, however, favors Solomon over David.

Joseph (or Asaf) ben Barakhya, Solomon's secretary, is a character from Arabic legend, where he is called "the father of medicine" and given a seat on the flying carpet. This "father of medicine" is not to be confused with Imhotep, "the father of medicine" in Egyptian legend.

The nameless first minister of Sheba appears as the queen's attendant or companion in the Tigre oral and the Amhara pictorial traditions of Ethiopia, though not, interestingly, in the official Ethiopian national epic. She and the queen have an Amazon flavor in Tigre, dressing in men's clothes and pretending to be men. They are unmasked and raped.

The Ethiopian national epic gives the merchant Tamrin complete credit for bringing Solomon and Sheba together. In earlier sources, no more credible intermediary is cited than a little talking bird.

The queen of Sheba has taken on many guises. Current archaeologists, favoring a Yemenite Sabaea, see her as a hard camel-rider of the Arabian desert. Hollywood has repeatedly depicted her as a sybaritic love princess. One revisionist historian, Immanuel Velikovsky, argues she was the half sister of King Solomon's Egyptian wife, and none other than the female pharaoh Hatshepsut; whence, egotistical and interested in her own power. Ethiopian legend has her a raped virgin. Current Jungian poetry describes Sheba as a reincarnate Hindu-Persian archetype, in love with the priest-king Melchizedek. The only man ever to write convincingly of King Solomon's mines—H. Rider Haggard—postulates a deathless, fair-skinned empress of the cannibals. Coptic and Axumite legends call her a cripple. The Koran says Sheba's throne was stolen by Solomon. The Bible and current Harlem jazz opera see her as a riddler and quester for truth. The Bible and current historians see her as a rich potentate on an economic mission. In Byzantine legend she is a sibyl. In Levantine Christianity, she is a symbol of the pagan world, or of the true church, honoring Christ in the person of Solomon or in the wood of the cross over which she stumbles. By Ethiopian law she is the ancestress of a Solomonic line of kings. In cabala, she will destroy Rome at the end of days. A medieval tavernkeeper painted her onto his signboard as Queen Goosefoot. She was a sun worshiper who converted, according to the Koran. She was the daughter of demons, or genii, or of a peri (fairy), say Arabic speakers. She was a Taoist holy person, writes a Sinologist from Berlin. She was the queen of the south, than whom even Solomon was not more wise—it is implied, in the Bible.

The legends of Arwé and the Tôbba, snakes or men whom Sheba killed for her throne, are Ethiopian and Arabian respectively. I learned of them from an Arab author quoted by a Russian writing a French book published recently in Cairo.

A Persian fable describes the queen of Sheba's parents as a Chinese king and a peri. It seemed logical to me to combine this with the little-known legend of Mu Wang, the tenth century B.C. Chinese king who traveled six thousand miles to see the "Queen Mother of the West."

My hypothesis that the queendom of Sheba was very large needs some defending, since I don't believe it has been suggested before. The New Testament refers to Sheba as "queen of the south," suggesting a wide area of dominion. She is also known by this title, Eteye aZeeb or "queen of the south," in Ethiopian oral tradition. Both Christian missionaries and Arab travelers have reported finding a Sheba tradition throughout the continent of Africa, west to the Congo and south to the Transvaal, "wherever gold is mined." Many concede a connection between Sheba and Ethiopia (also known as Abyssinia), but these place names may connote a larger area than is usually thought. Sociologists say that in classical times "Ethiopia" meant all of black Africa. And in the Middle Ages "Abyssinia" covered about a third of the continent. Working with current maps, I found more than forty cities, villages, rivers, and other geographical names containing the linguistic root Sh-B or S-B, concentrated over southern Arabia and the whole long eastern half of Africa.

The question of the Sheban land area has political implications. The Ethiopian national epic of A.D. 1290 lists the boundaries of Sheba in a prominent place; the difficulty is that the terms they used as geographical referents are now obsolete. The Russians are excavating for Sheba in communist South Yemen. In the United States a Sheba consciousness is part of a black cultural renaissance. Who wouldn't want to establish a connection with this brilliant queen? Or with Sheba's famed gold wealth, often equated with "the gold of Ophir" (Africa?) and doubtless comparable, if not identical, with the wealth of King Solomon's famous mines.

It seemed reasonable to me to picture a Sheban empire as large as the perimeter of legendary diffusion (considering that the transmission had to be oral and nonelectronic), with capitals at two foci, where the legend is most highly developed. There is little disagreement that this would describe Axum in Ethiopia and Marib in Arabia, not far distant from one another, and known as spiritual and economic centers respectively. Sociologists write that the ancient monarchs of Ethiopia were "peripatetic."

Sheba's contention that there were "twelve hundred million" people in her empire reflects Arab mythology. The figure is laughingly rejected by modern scholars. It struck me, though, that this number is of the same order of magnitude as Homer's estimate of the Greeks who fought at Troy (112,500,000).

The word "Sheba" (interchangeable with "Saba") has many etymologies. In Hebrew it means "old one," and "captor." In Arabic, "merchants." In Ethiopian, "men." Most interesting of all, the Greek dictionary defines "sabba" as *pudendum mulieribus*. This bit of news supports my theory that the Sheban empire was ruled by women.

Many historians agree that women played a large role in government in the prehistoric ages, especially in the Near East, where there is evidence of their preeminence in economics, the family, and religion. To my knowledge, however, the queen of Sheba has never been discussed in these terms. So I have suggested that the Biblical Sheba was a matriarch who consciously enacted in her country the kind of political changes that occurred in many different places over a period of a thousand years or more, resulting finally in worldwide patriarchy.

213

The most telling evidence for this is in the Ethiopian national epic, where the queen of Sheba, after visiting Solomon and bearing his son, decrees "there shall no more be queens in Ethiopia, but only a man."

Somewhat analogously, the queen of Sheba incident in the Koran is usually interpreted to mean that she converted to Solomon's religion.

There is also mythological evidence. Oral tradition in Ethiopia links the queen with the end of the snake cult. But snake cults are frequently associated by scholars with priestesses and gynecocracy. Similarly, a Jewish legend credits King Solomon with "decreeing the death of the serpent."

Which gets into the question of the queen's bad ankle. It was incumbent upon me to deal with the very pervasive and widespread legend (though not found in the Bible, the Koran, Glory of Kings, or masonic writings) that there was something wrong with the queen of Sheba's foot, feet, or legs. The mildest form this motif takes is in Jewish legend from around the time of the Koran. There, an innocuous Koranic hint that Solomon tricked Sheba into lifting her gown, and in showing her legs she embarrassed herself, is developed into an indictment of hairy legs. Later Arabic legend carried this further, saying that because she was *sa-ir*, "hairy," she was also *se-ir*, a "goat demon," and it passed into tradition that the queen had a foot deformed like a goat's foot. Other Arabic legends, meanwhile, explained away even the alleged hairiness, saying it was an invention by her enemies in the Jewish court, who didn't want her and Solomon to get together and generate too much power.

But the well had been poisoned. Depilatory formulae were discussed. Christian legend gave her an ass's or a goose's foot, which was miraculously cured when she had a sibylline vision of Christ. In 1967 an avant-garde film featured the queen of Sheba shaving her legs.

I despaired of understanding the source of all this mischief, when I came across an oral tradition from Tigre which had something unique to say about the queen's foot problem. The Tigre informant had told a Swedish missionary that Sheba's hooflike extremity was engendered by the blood (or bones) of a dragon slain by her (or her father). And that her motive in going to see Solomon was to draw upon his wisdom for a cure. I thought this was an important clue. If the serpent, snake, dragon motif is associated with female power, then Sheba's physical imperfection can be seen as a symbol of her divided mind with respect to female rule, from which condition Solomon "cures" her.

But another explanation for the problematic lower limb may be even more plausible. Anthropologists say that ritual laming was practiced at some stage in ancient history or prehistory as a concomitant to the coronation of a king. Since a beautiful Persian legend speaks of the queen of Sheba

214

choosing at puberty whether to belong to the world of spirits or the world of humans, I thought her decision to accept a laming at this point, and become therefore human, might tie things up neatly.

What would an ancient matriarchy have been like? Many models have been suggested. In constructing Sheba, I made use of elements in the theories of Friedrich Engels, J. J. Bachofen, and Charlotte Perkins Gilman. In *The Origin of the Family, Private Property, and the State,* Engels describes the "punalua," a primitive kinship system involving group marriage. In *Myth, Religion, and Mother Right,* Bachofen hypothesizes that social life in the prehistoric Near East was "Aphroditean," or promiscuous. And Gilman theorizes, in *Women and Economics,* that the greater size of modern men is a result of selective breeding.

But the point about sexual synchronization is my own deduction from primary sources. Examining published and unpublished translations of an Aramaic text written soon after the time of Christ, which the masons as well as the Jews have taken care to preserve, I found the statement that Sheba sent ahead of her to Jerusalem "six thousand young men and young women, all of them born in the same year and the same month, the same day and the same hour," of the same stature and dressed alike. I thought, reading literally, how could this be possible? For Sheba to have been able to collect six thousand persons born simultaneously, either her nation must have been extremely numerous—only a population of two billion, at today's birthrates, could fill such a quota—or, as I thought more likely, her social organization must have permitted of simultanous procreation. For there to have been large-scale simultanous procreation, either Sheba must have been a tyranny of the worst sort, which I could not believe, or else all or most of the women's sexual cycles must have been in synchrony. Given such a state of affairs, it was easy to imagine that women's collective power in other areas besides the sexual was also significant. And wouldn't this be sufficient to explain a woman-run civilization? I certainly preferred it to the more dreadful hypotheses about ancient matriarchies.

Solomon's magic flying carpet is an Arabian invention, usually made of green silk, the Islamic holy color. Solomon flies around the world on it, picking up planetary information. One Arabic story about his meeting with Sheba has him flying to Mecca, and being told there about the land of Sheba, and "the largest and most superb city ever constructed by the hand of man." This is Marib, splendid by reason of its system of dikes and canals.

The oldest Jewish version of Solomon's discovery of Sheba omits the flying carpet and puts Solomon instead at a banquet, "merry with wine," being entertained by an array of unchained animals. This story bears one striking similarity to the Arabic tale: from Solomon's performing zoo, as from the company of birds which fly over the magic carpet, only the hoopoe is missing.

To arrive at the librarian's analysis of Solomon's carpet trick, I fused the Arabian flight with the Jewish festivity, and interpreted both according to a twelfth-century Sufi fable about birds.

The cabalists' version of Solomon's flight has him on eagle back (traditionally the enemy of the Arab-favored hoopoe), soaring "behind the black mountain in cloud and storm," to check out the secrets of witchcraft with a male and a female demon chained together there. This is obviously a different trip, so I assigned it to the troubled period following his loss of Sheba.

Although Solomon's marriage to the daughter of a pharaoh is related in the Bible, few details are given. The Talmud says that she brought to Solomon's house a star canopy for the bed and a thousand musical instruments each with its own god. Standard Egyptological sources list scores of instruments in use at the time, and indicate that they were made of gold and silver, and played by women. It was for Dorothy Siegal (M.Mus., Yale) and me to suggest which gods might have inhered in which instruments, on the basis of the personalities of the members of the modern orchestra.

But her stupendous astronomical and musical gifts aside, I wondered why Solomon chose to marry the pharaoh's daughter. I found no speculation on this question even though, historically, she was the first such pharaonic princess to be given out of the country in marriage, and though there was no comparable Israeli-Egyptian alliance from Solomon's time until 1979.

Masonic sources confirmed my hunch that Solomon was interested in Egyptian building technology. They report that eighty thousand builders came to Israel as part of his Egyptian bride's dowry, citing two early Church fathers for this information. Jewish legend also reports a gift of Egyptian builders, with a wise-guy retort: saying that Solomon could see the Egyptians were all about to die, and sent them back to the pharaoh with Jewish-made shrouds. I took this anecdote nearly at face value, making the builders advanced in years. But considering the necrotheism of old Egypt, it may have more levels of meaning to plumb.

Jewish legend credits Solomon with calendar reform, and the reform outlined is the one still in use in the Jewish calendar. I emphasized the ambiguity of the Hebrew *sod hebor*, which dictionaries define both as "the science of fixing the calendar," and "(joc.) the secret of pregnancy (when to become pregnant)." To make matters worse, the former of the two idioms is called the "white" science or secret.

The theft of Sheba's throne occurs in the Koran, where it is one of the main incidents of Solomon and Sheba's meeting. Solomon's scribe is said to fetch it more quickly than a lurking *afreet* (the ghost of one who died by violence). Having stolen it, Solomon tests Sheba by asking whether it is hers. She passes the test by answering cagily, "Very like mine." In Persian legend and some Italian paintings Sheba's throne takes on increased significance: there it is described as a "parade bed throne," with the enormous dimensions I have given. In the Bible and Jewish legend there is a lot of material about the zoomorphic machinery of Solomon's throne, and in the Song of Songs is mentioned Solomon's palanquin "inlaid wth love by the daughters of Jerusalem." No connection is made in Jewish sources between Solomon's throne and Sheba's. It seemed clear to me, however, that the symbolism of the throne means to say that Solomon tried to appropriate for himself (unsuccessfully, as it turned out) Sheba's sexual power.

That Sheba asked Solomon "hard questions" lies at the heart of the Biblical story of their meeting. Her questions are not given. I have suggested that the epigrammatic wisdom in the Book of Proverbs, traditionally attributed to Solomon, could have been inspired by the Sheban dialogues.

Over the centuries Jewish folklorists have compiled a list of twenty questions Sheba may have asked Solomon. Arabic sources list about another half dozen. I rejected most of these as not suiting my purposes. The answers "oil" (really: naphtha), "flax," and "kohl" are from Jewish sources, though I changed the questions. Two other riddles I used come verbatim from Jewish tradition: the days of pregnancy riddle and the enclosure with ten openings riddle. I supplemented these riddles with sayings attributed to Solomon by gnostics of an Omar Khayyám sect and by the ideologue of the whirling dervishes.

That Sheba made Solomon differentiate between the sexes is found in Jewish, Arabic, and Ethiopian sources. That Solomon perhaps failed in the task is implied by the fact that three traditions report the one problem, but three unlike solutions. The situation appears under varying lights, from an intellectual riddle to a technological challenge to a rape. Invariably, Solomon makes the distinction on the basis of a nuance of behavior. The Jews discuss male versus female dispositions of clothing. The Arabs discuss male versus female modes of handwashing. The Ethiopians stipulate that males eat meat, bread, and beer, while females prefer fruit and sweets.

217

It was my idea to connect the legends of sex differentiation with the legend of the six thousand boys and girls of like stature, and dressed alike.

I am intuitively sure that the Song of Songs was a love poem written by or for Solomon and Sheba. But this is not the accepted view. Jews and Christians both identify the lovers in the poem as God and his people or, failing that, as two male antagonists, Solomon and a country boy, competing for the love of a country girl. Some scholars date the work as late as eight hundred years after Solomon. Traditional Jewish scholarship does, however, place it in the time of Solomon, on the basis of its tone, a reference to it in the Book of Kings, and references within the poem to the city of Tirzah and to the "horse in pharaoh's chariots."

I have included several excerpts from my own translation of the Song of Songs. For example, I have translated, "I am a cavewoman and a noblewoman . . . My beloved is the first man on earth and he is radiant." These are the lines which the King James renders poetically, but I think incorrectly, as, "I am black but comely . . . My beloved is white and ruddy."

That white = radiant, and ruddy = Adamic, can be shown with no difficulty. The most interesting disagreement concerns the Hebrew word *shkorh*, which conventional translations render as "black." First of all, *sh-* can be an introductory particle, meaning "that." And *korh* in Hebrew means "noblewoman," a feminine form of "cave," and . . . "white." I felt that, though the queen of Sheba may indeed have had a shade of skin darker than Solomon's, being from the south, that she probably did not have, in those days of the greatness of her empire, an apologetic race consciousness about it. Further, I wondered whether *korh* might possibly be related to the Greek Kóre, "maid," daughter of Demeter, the Eleusinian mystery girl.

The Song of Songs was the last book to be canonized as part of the Old Testament. And of the rabbi who handed down the canonizing resolution, it is said that he entered into the garden of the esoteric doctrine and died of ecstasy.

Sheba does not exist for the Talmudic rabbis, as has been noted. However there is in the Talmud a metaphor of the holy arc as a bed. The Talmud says: "For this bed is too short that two neighbors may rule therein together," with specific reference to the arc of the covenant; and the modern editor explains that this means there is no room for both "God and the idol."

Moshailama (Moçailama) and Shedja are characters from fifteenth-century

218

Arabic love literature, not usually identified with Solomon and Sheba. But I noticed that their story was analogous, and their names cognate.

The queen of Sheba has been associated with narcotics at least since the bohemian liberation of the nineteenth century, and recently John Updike invoked her name to the same purpose. There is good reason. Qat, a mild narcotic, has been in use in Yemen for untold centuries, according to *The New York Times*. The narcotic mandrake, mentioned in the Song of Songs, is still in use today. But the most convincing evidence that Sheba was skilled in the use of drugs is found in the Bible itself. The King James translation reports that the queen gave to Solomon a quantity and type of "spice" never before or since seen in Jerusalem. The Hebrew word translated "spice," and suggestive even at that, is *bsm*, which *Bsm* can also be translated "perfume, flavor, intoxicant," and "to be tipsy, drunken."

Egypt was probably involved with even harder stuff. Unusually potent opium is grown there today. An Egyptian opium called Thēbē was produced at the ancient priestly city of Thebes, according to Webster.

Archaeology is strangely ambivalent on the subject of the Temple Solomon built. A nineteenth-century history of Phoenicia confirms the collegial relationship ascribed in the Bible to King Solomon and King Hiram of Tyre, and goes on to say that the Temple in Jerusalem was built by Phoenician workers, using stone blocks as large as 25 feet by 18 feet by 12 feet and weighing, as I have mentioned in the narrative, as much as a hundred tons. Excavations in Palestine are cited. However the leading twentieth-century Biblical archaeologists feel that no certain traces of Solomon's Temple have yet been unearthed. The prime difficulty is that the site has been enthusiastically built over at least three times—by Jews returning from Babylon, by Christians, and by Moslems.

Elaborate descriptions of Solomon's Temple in the Biblical books of Kings, Chronicles, and Ezekiel (who, tradition says, measured the ruins) have led many people to make sketches of what the first Temple may have looked like. These are astonishingly varied. My favorites were done by a Harvard-educated Swedenborgian minister, Timothy Otis Paine, in a gigantic and meticulously documented tome, and it is his suggestions that I have followed wherever I have described the structure.

Supposing that huge stones were used in the construction of the Temple, how were they cut, lifted, and finished? This question is asked about the pyramid blocks, and to answer it archaeologists imagine a system of ramps and log cylinder wheels. Limestone (though not granite) can be easily cut when still underground and wet.

In the oldest Jewish tradition the rabbis evoke a supernatural referral system to explain the apparently lost technological feat of cutting stones. The Talmud says that Solomon's rabbis told him to consult a male and a female demon chained together, who told him to consult the prince of demons (or prince of the sea), who told him the secret was an entity called the "shamir" (a borer worm? an insect? some kind of wood or seed? a green stone?), which was in the custody of the woodpecker (or hoopoe, or rokh), which was wont to drop it into the crevasses of the big rocks, where it took root (?) and eventually cracked them open of its own accord. So Solomon, it is said, tricked the "shamir" away from its custodian, and used it to build the Temple.

Now this is a very great mystery. The masons say the lost technological secret of the "shamir" (which they also call "shermah") is greater than the mystery of the signs, the tokens, and the passwords. There are some who would introduce modern technology at this point to explain the ancient mystery. Mainstream scientists call this "paradoxicalism." I call it a *machina ex deā*. All one has to deny is evolution, to believe that guiding the Jews across the desert, or lodged in the arc of the covenant, or helping build the Temple, was a dry cell battery, or a radio. Well, but I didn't want to go this route, so I focused my attention on the little bird which, some say, committed suicide when it gave up its secret.

A possible key to the conundrum is the report in the Koran and concurrent Jewish legend that the hoopoe discovered Sheba, and announced her and her country to Solomon, and delivered his message of invitation or threat to her. In other words, the creature that introduces king and queen to each other is also one of the prime candidates for custodian of the Temple building secret. Beneath the rabbinic code is a simple pagan thought: love is necessary for work. And in the process of discovering this secret, the troubled king must learn the lessons of a couple united, and of an undefinable mite dropped into a crevasse.

Solomon's prince or king of demons may be none other than Hermes/ Mercury, or (that is) Thoth. But in Jewish tradition he is called only Asmodeus, or Ashmedai, meaning The Cursed. Talmudically, this devil plays a minor role in the building of the Temple, juxtaposed with agents of the good, but a major role in Solomon's later downfall. A prominent living Jewish scholar has suggested that Ashmedai is (a) Hadad of Edom, and (b) the child whom Solomon juridically suggested be split in two.

The epithet "satan" is used as a common noun in the Biblical story of Solomon, to describe both Hadad of Edom and Rezon the outlaw of Damascus.

*   *   *

In placing Sheba's arrival in Jerusalem prior to the completion of the Temple, I have followed masonic tradition.

One notable nonmasonic source also asserts that "the queen of Sheba saw the Temple of the Lord being builded." That is *The Testament of Solomon*, a powerful short work extant in six or seven Greek editions, which Jews consider to have a core of Solomonic material overlaid with Christian elements, Catholics call apocryphal, and Protestants classify as pseudepigrapha.

In the Bible, very specific dates are given for the building of the Temple, both in terms of Solomon's regime and of the long-previous Israelite coming out of Egypt. But no specific dates are given for the visit of the queen of Sheba. In the order of verses, her arrival follows Solomon's marriage to the pharaoh's daughter and precedes his marriages to the hundreds of other women; I have retained this order and, indeed, emphasized its significance. Her arrival is also placed after the building of the Temple. However, since the Temple section is so long and her section so short, the verses might have been arranged this way for stylistic purposes. Then, too, the Biblical order of verses is not always strictly chronological: the character Joab is slain in Kings 2, and recalled to action in a flashback in Kings 11.

Students of high school plane geometry learn that it was Pythagoras who discovered that the sum of the squares of the sides of a right triangle is equal to the square of the hypotenuse. However the seven-volume *Encyclopedia of Freemasonry* credits this discovery to Hiram the Temple architect, and I thought this interesting enough to bear repeating.

In the Bible the building of the Temple proceeds smoothly. The nationalities, numbers, and areas of responsibility of the workmen are given. Jeroboam is a young overseer rising in the ranks, whose ambitions finally come to threaten Solomon. Political categories are not used, but enough information is given about Jeroboam's later ascension to the throne of Israel to see he was a populist and an opportunist.

The Testament of Solomon seems to suggest that there were labor difficulties in the building of the Temple, and to analyze how Solomon overcame them. The only trouble, for us, is that it speaks in the archaic terms of demonology. To wit: a demon (flea? mosquito? daimon of ambition?) bites Solomon's overseer on the neck, bringing all work on the Temple to a halt. At the king's command, many additional demons and supernatural entities appear, each threatening specific physical and psychic harms. Solomon succeeds in discovering from them all the necessary practical and magical antidotes. He thus harnesses their power for the Temple work, and in the last scene there is the panorama of Beelzeboul sawing marble, and so on. I thought it sounded like a strike, organized and broken.

There is a Jewish tradition that after the Temple was dedicated, "the

221

workmen died off, lest they build similar structures for the heathen and their gods." And the death by assassination of Hiram the architect is a central theme in the masonic tradition. But the Jews don't speak of the death of Hiram, and the masons don't speak of the deaths of the Temple workmen. It is as if they were on different sides.

Combining both teachings, I concluded that there must have been an all-out battle at the time of the completion of the Temple, perhaps precipitated by the violent death of the architect. The names of possible assassins come from standard masonic sources. One particularly picturesque account of this murder is given by Gérard de Nerval in his *Voyage en Orient*, which he says he heard behind the Bayezid Mosque in Istanbul.

Masonic sources take more than one line on the death of the architect. Sometimes they blame Solomon squarely: "A marriage had been arranged between King Solomon and the queen of Sheba, but when the Queen beheld the builder of the Temple her admiration was transferred to him; which so enraged the monarch that the murder of Hiram Abiff was the result of a conspiracy initiated by King Solomon himself." At other times they suggest a more mythic, even impersonal view of the event, saying that Hiram was a "living incarnation of Adonis, who was offered up as a Consecration Sacrifice at the completion of the great Temple at Jerusalem . . . in order that the new Temple might stand firm for ever." I attributed the latter sentiment to King Hiram of Tyre, himself a character in masonic legend, since historians seem to agree that human sacrifice was practiced in his country.

And since archaeologists have verified Solomon's use of slave labor, I thought it logical that the slaves be involved in some way in the uprising at the Temple. I also felt it was likely that this masonic/labor battle would have had an (unsuccessful) collectivizing thrust.

Jews generally believe that Solomon wrote the Song of Songs, Proverbs, and Ecclesiastes, and rabbis add that these books were written in his youth, maturity, and old age respectively. The *Book of the Acts of Solomon* is mentioned several times in the Bible, but has never been found. The long list of other books I have attributed to Solomon do in fact exist in Hebrew, Arabic, Greek, Latin, and German editions, and are held to be of Solomonic authorship by Arabic tradition. The Arabs also believe that Solomon invented the Arabic and Syriac scripts.

Solomon's medical knowledge is widely credited. Whether Solomon practiced magic or not is a point of contention, with the cabalists saying yes, and mainstream rabbis saying that he put magical books behind his throne for safekeeping, but didn't use them. An argument can be made that Solomon's putative knowledge of "demons"—little flying things that make people ill and can be fought back with chemical substances—is nothing more magical than ancient medicine.

The passage I have called "a book" is my own translation of the short section in Kings which tells the Solomon and Sheba story. The only substantive disagreement I have with the beautiful King James translation occurs at the end of the passage. King James: "And King Solomon gave unto the queen of Sheba all her desire, whatsoever she asked, beside that which Solomon gave her of his royal bounty." The last four words translate the Hebrew *chyd*, which can be literally "by his hand." But *chyd* can also mean "calamity, disaster, misfortune," and I think this negative meaning makes better sense of the abrupt sentence that follows: "So she turned and went to her own country, she and her servants." It would also confirm the masonic sense of the story.

Orthodox Jews believe the first few books of the Bible were written by Moses five centuries prior to Solomon's time. Reform rabbis and archaeologists date the writing of the Bible at approximately 350 years after Solomon, in the turmoil around the fall of the Temple. I have followed the view of the Jerusalem librarian of a worldwide Jewish fraternal organization, B'nai B'rith, who quotes several scholars to the effect that the Bible was most likely written in or around the court of King Solomon—and if so, then by Abiathar, the exiled high priest.

Whether Solomon lived before or after the writing of the Bible seems to have a bearing on how he is historically assessed. The Talmud says that Solomon disobeyed several provisions in the Biblical book of Deuteronomy (i.e., not to multiply to himself wives or horses, or amass gold), and that therein he sinned. But a gnostic viewpoint holds that the book of Deuteronomy was written for the express purpose of retroactively condemning Solomon, and suppressing a Solomonic cult (a Jewish twenty-second amendment).

Sheba's story about the unicorn in Eden comes from Jewish legend. But Solomon is also heavily involved in the Garden of Eden myth. The garden metaphor for the body appears throughout his Song of Songs. The waters of Sheba, like the wood Solomon used for the Temple, are said in many legends to have come from Eden. To this day many Arabs in Jerusalem believe that King Solomon is buried underneath a certain jasper slab called "the Stone (or Gate) of Eden." Gnostics say that the Adam and Eve story in Genesis was written with an anti-Solomonic purpose, to point out the dangers of knowledge.

The pharaoh's daughter's discussion of the pyramids is my interpretation of standard Egyptological material. Sheba's discussion of the pyramids is based on old dictionaries, art histories, and lectures given at a meeting of an archaeological society in New York City in 1974. Hiram's pyramidology comes from a Rudolf Steiner publication; the story he tells about the relation of the pyramids to the flood comes from the legend of Enoch as developed in freemasonry.

Arabians and Ethiopians believe there was a son of Solomon and Sheba, and they call him David II and Son of the Wise Man. In Ethiopia he is also called Menyelek or Menelik; around Axum, in particular, the name Other-Self is mentioned. An 1880 Protestant yearbook in German uniquely gives the name of this child as Bel-Ami, which I have translated as I Chose My People.

I have left the father of the queen of Sheba's son unnamed, in the spirit of ancient matriarchy. But since we no longer live in a matriarchy, there are some contradictory theories and hard feelings on this score now. Above all, the Ethiopian constitution of 1955, by declaring their kings to be descended from Solomon and Sheba, almost has the character of an intergovernmental paternity suit. According to the thirteenth-century epic upon which the ancestral claim is based, Solomon never knew Sheba was pregnant. Glory of Kings says she came to him a virgin, was tricked into his bed one time, and immediately thereafter departed.

In the Amharic pictorial and Tigre oral traditions of Ethiopia, Solomon begot sons on both the queen of Sheba and her attendant-companion. He slept with the queen first, and then with her attendant, taking them both either by a ruse or by not-entirely-resisted force, and (according to the pictures) in sight of each other. In these versions the attendant and her son are portrayed as darker-skinned than the queen and her son.

There is also a written tradition—at core masonic, but with some imaginative elements—that Sheba rejected Solomon and bore a child to Hiram. This theory is real anathema to an Ethiopian; one French romantic suggested the dispute be solved by letting the Ethiopians battle it out with the Ali-sect Muslims in a unionized Turkish opium-smokers' café.

I don't believe anyone before has suggested that the queen of Sheba had carnal knowledge both of Solomon and of Hiram, though polyandry is well-attested in ancient Arabia and Africa. Of course, this would leave the paternity question still unsolved, and insoluble.

The gold-encased pyramid of Solomon's dreams derives from Arabic legend. It is said that Solomon on his flying carpet discovered a doorless palace, guarded by 700-, 900-, and 1300-year-old eagles, which he entered and where he had the kind of experiences I have summarized. A certain king is named, who gave Solomon the final message of enlightenment/

disillusionment. More realistic teachings speak of the son of Harun al-Rashid, who in A.D. 825 broke into the great pyramid of Egypt for the first time, presumably, since it was built. Inside he expected to find all the dazzling riches, jewels, medicines, charms, and sciences of an antediluvian Arab king of the earth; and the name of this king is the same as the king named in the Solomon legend of the eagle palace. It should be noticed that the pyramids were built something like thirteen hundred years before Solomon's time.

Scholars say the original source of all the stories about Solomon's (or Sheba's) ring is the *Testament of Solomon*. Though I'm not very fond of the theme, I can't help but feel this is the same ring that Aladdin rubbed, that was wrested briefly from the Rhine Maidens, and that most recently J. R. R. Tolkien put into the hands of the Hobbits.

Biblically, Solomon had over seven hundred wives, three hundred concubines, and some problems with religion toward the end of his administration. Talmudically, the problem is split personality, with a demon in Solomon's likeness on the throne, and the real Solomon wandering the countryside telling people he is king and not being believed. Arabic legend also sends Solomon into exile, but only for forty days, compared to the Talmud's three years.

The Talmud deals with this situation on three levels. First of all, Solomon's name comes up in the middle of a very folksy discussion of sanity tests and delirium therapies, a few of which I have cited. Second, the Talmud relates that the Sanhedrin met to discuss Solomon's fitness. This supreme court of seventy elders called witnesses, including former general Benaiah, who testified that he was being ignored, and the women of Solomon's harem, who testified to the violation of "family purity" (a concept still important in orthodox Judaism). The precise nature of the false Solomon's sexual violation is obscure. Menstrual cohabitation, for one thing. Beyond that, the passage in Aramaic is so subtle or taboo it doesn't survive translation into English. The English Talmud says he called for his mother. The authoritative *Jewish Encyclopedia*, referring to the same passage, says he attacked his mother. Finally, the Sanhedrin, after accusing the king of keeping his socks on to conceal the fact that he had bird feet like a demon, cures him, i.e., put the real Solomon back on the throne, by means of a ring and chain inscribed with the tetragrammation. Solomon is reinstated, again king of Judah and Israel, but no longer king "over the unseen world."

On a third level, the Talmudic rabbis, like the early Church fathers, debate Solomon's salvation. They describe themselves, a millennium afterward, trying to pass eternal judgment on him, as they have done on all the other kings. But supernatural signs keep preventing them. Finally they decide that judgment will be passed on this one only in paradise, and only by kings.

The name of Sheba appears only once in all the work of Shakespeare. That is on the last page of the last play he wrote, which is also the last of his ten history plays, and thus on the borderline of his contemporaneity. A child has just been born and is being baptized; it is Elizabeth, Shakespeare's own patron of the arts. The queen is blessed by the archbishop, and the brilliance of her reign predicted. "She shall be—but few now living can behold that goodness—a pattern to all princes living with her, and all that shall succeed: Saba was never more covetous of wisdom and fair virtue than this pure soul shall be . . ."

ACKNOWLEDGMENTS

Fιrst of all, I would like to give special thanks to Steven A. Kraft, who read the manuscript at an early stage and gave me invaluable guidance; and to my researchers Jeffrey L. Wolloch, Oxford University, and Christian Filstrup of the Oriental Division of the New York Public Library who, with Mrs. Filstrup, made the Arabic materials accessible to me.

Next, I would like to acknowledge gratefully the assistance I received in many forms from Michael Abram, Rick Applegate, Associate Rabbi Herschel Cohen of Lincoln Square Synagogue, Pauline Conboy, Rabbi Dovid Deen of Brooklyn, Rabbi Meyer Fund of Brooklyn College, Nina Haft, Matana Cohen Hemingway, Isaac's Reggae Disco, Rabbi Wolfe Kelman of the Jewish Theological Seminary, Rabbi Alan B. Lettofsky of Jerusalem, Josh Lewin, Robert Shulman, Emory Ed Taylor of the Harlem Opera Society, Ruth Ann Taylor, Sheila Thornton, Joe Truchsess, and my friends on Spanishtown Road.

Finally, I should like to thank, though I can never really do so adequately, my father Judge Seymour R. Levine; the foe of my adversity Mike Matthews, president of the Electro-Harmonix company; and my agent and friend Elaine Markson, as well as editors Joyce Engelson and Anne Knauerhase at Richard Marek Publishers, who let me work in the luxury of their wisdom and trust.